FOALS IN THE FIELD

The rain beat down. The tarpaulin flapped loose, waving wildly in the wind. Lightning split the sky.

Mandy grabbed James's arm. 'Look!' she said.

The whole roof was moving now, sliding inwards.

Mandy snatched the jumper. 'Take Dash to the field,' she said to James. 'I'm going after Nick. He'll never get Dot out on his own.'

James made a dive for her but Dash plunged, his hooves clattering on the cobbles of the stableyard. James lurched sideways.

'Mandy!' he yelled. 'You can't go in there. You heard what Nick said.'

But Mandy didn't hear him above the roar of the wind, the pounding of the rain. She was flying towards the stables, plunging through the door. The sound of creaking timbers filled the stables as she searched for Nick.

Animal Ark series

1 Kittens in the Kitchen
2 Pony in the Porch
3 Puppies in the Pantry
4 Goat in the Garden
5 Hedgehogs in the Hall
6 Badger in the Basement
7 Cub in the Cupboard
8 Piglet in a Playpen
9 Owl in the Office
10 Lamb in the Laundry
11 Bunnies in the Bathroom
12 Donkey on the Doorstep
13 Hamster in a Hamper
14 Goose on the Loose
15 Calf in the Cottage
16 Koalas in a Crisis
17 Wombat in the Wild
18 Roo on the Rock
19 Squirrels in the School
20 Guinea-pig in the Garage
21 Fawn in the Forest
22 Shetland in the Shed
23 Swan in the Swim
24 Lion by the Lake
25 Elephants in the East
26 Monkeys on the Mountain
27 Dog at the Door
28 Foals in the Field
Seal on the Shore
Sheepdog in the Snow
Kitten in the Cold
Fox in the Frost

LUCY DANIELS

Foals *in the* Field

a division of Hodder Headline plc

Special thanks to Helen Magee
Thanks also to C. J. Hall, B.Vet.Med., M.R.C.V.S., for reviewing the veterinary information contained in this book.

First published in Great Britain in 1997
by Hodder Children's Books

10 9 8 7 6 5 4 3 2 1

A Catalogue record for this book is available from the British Library

ISBN 0 340 69949 3

Typeset by Avon Dataset Ltd, Bidford-on-Avon, Warks

Printed and bound in Great Britain by
Clays Ltd, St Ives plc, Bungay, Suffolk

Hodder Children's Books
a division of Hodder Headline plc
338 Euston Road
London NW1 3BH

One

Mandy Hope sat at the kitchen table at Animal Ark, watching the sun glinting off her mother's row of shiny brass pans. The warm spring air blew in at the open window, ruffling the red checked curtains.

Mandy could hear her father talking on the telephone in the hall. Mandy's parents were both vets in the village of Welford. Animal Ark was their home as well as their surgery.

'I wonder who that is,' she said dreamily. Mandy was always interested in the patients her mother and father took care of.

Emily Hope put a bowl of fluffy scrambled

eggs on the kitchen table and smiled. 'Whoever it is, I hope they don't keep your dad much longer,' she said. 'Otherwise these eggs will get cold.'

'Mmm, can I start?' Mandy asked.

'Go ahead,' said Mrs Hope. She cocked her head. 'That's him finished.'

Mandy scooped a pile of scrambled eggs on to her plate as her father came into the kitchen.

'That was Nick Summers on the phone,' he said to his wife as he sat down at the table.

Mandy looked at her dad, concern on her face. 'Bessie is all right, isn't she?' she asked.

Bessie was Nick's brood mare up at Drysdale Farm. She was in foal and due to give birth in a few weeks. And, even more exciting – she was expecting twins!

Mr Hope ruffled his daughter's fair hair and poured himself a cup of tea from the blue and white striped pot.

'Of course she is,' he replied. 'Nick is just a bit worried about her, that's all. She's been restless.'

Mrs Hope looked up. 'How restless?' she asked.

Mr Hope shrugged. 'Nick says she's been lying

down and standing up since early morning,' he said. 'She just can't settle.'

'What does that mean?' Mandy asked.

Mrs Hope looked concerned. 'Sometimes when a mare is near to giving birth she gets very uncomfortable,' she said. 'She moves about, lies down, stands up.'

'You mean Bessie might be foaling early?' said Mandy.

'She might be showing signs of restlessness just because she's carrying twins,' said Mr Hope.

'I hope so,' Mrs Hope said. 'Nick has got enough troubles without premature foals to look after.'

'Mrs Ponsonby says Nick has taken on more than he can chew at Drysdale,' said Mandy, munching a slice of toast.

Emily Hope laughed. 'That sounds just like Mrs Ponsonby,' she replied.

Mrs Ponsonby was the bossiest woman in Welford. She was a leading light in the Welford village Women's Institute. If anybody set up a committee, Mrs Ponsonby was bound to be on it – no matter what it was for!

'She's always poking her nose into other people's business,' said Mandy.

Fiona *is* Mrs Ponsonby's niece,' Mrs Hope reminded her. 'Mrs Ponsonby is quite worried about her. She says Fiona is wearing herself out working up at Drysdale every weekend.'

'But Fiona *wants* to help Nick with the farm so that they can get married,' Mandy declared. 'I think he's wonderful, wanting to raise horses.'

'Mrs Ponsonby doesn't think raising horses is a proper job,' said Emily Hope.

'She's wrong there,' said Adam Hope. 'It's one of the hardest jobs there is.'

'Oh, I'm really looking forward to seeing Bessie's foals,' said Mandy. 'But I hope they don't come *too* soon – for her sake.'

'It won't be easy for Bessie giving birth to twins,' said Emily Hope.

'Just imagine – twin foals!' exclaimed Mandy.

'Double the work,' said Mrs Hope. 'Nick *has* taken on a lot with that old farm. I hope he can manage two foals.'

Mandy looked at her mum. Emily Hope's bright red hair was tied back with a green scarf that matched her eyes.

'I bet you're glad I'm not twins,' she said.

'Now that really would be double trouble,' Mr Hope joked.

Mandy smiled. Adam and Emily Hope weren't her natural parents. Mandy's own mother and father had been killed in a car crash when she was a baby and the Hopes had adopted her. Mandy had never known her real parents, but that didn't worry her. Adam and Emily Hope were the best parents anybody could have.

'I said I'd go up and have a look at Bessie after breakfast,' said Adam Hope. 'I'm going that way anyway. I've got to look in on Tom Hapwell at Twyford.'

Mandy jiggled about on her chair. 'Can I come? Please, Dad,' she begged.

'I thought you and James were going to work on your project this morning,' Emily Hope reminded her.

'School work on a Saturday!' Mr Hope said. 'You and James must be turning over a new leaf.'

James was Mandy's best friend. They cycled to school in Walton together every day. He was a year younger than her and in a different class at school but they had persuaded their teachers to let them work on their local history project together. James and his Labrador, Blackie, were always round at Animal Ark. James liked animals almost as much as Mandy did.

Mandy groaned. 'Oh, so we were,' she said. Then she brightened. 'Wait a minute. Drysdale Farm is pretty old, isn't it, Dad?'

Mr Hope nodded. 'At least a couple of hundred years,' he said.

'That's all right then,' said Mandy. 'Our project is about Welford and the surrounding area as it was in olden times. Two hundred years is definitely olden times. James can come too and we can make it part of our project. I'll just give him a ring and get him to bring his camera and the Ordnance Survey map. I'll still have time to clean out Scrap's cage and see how he's getting on.'

Mandy jumped off her chair and made a dive for the door.

'Wait a minute,' cried her dad. 'I haven't said *you* can come, never mind James!'

Mandy put her head on one side. 'Oh, Dad, you wouldn't say no.'

Adam Hope raised his eyebrows until they almost disappeared under his dark hair. 'I suppose I wouldn't,' he said, smiling. 'OK, go on then.'

'Softie!' exclaimed Emily Hope to her husband.

Mandy made a dash for the phone. It was usually easier to get round her dad than her mum – and she really did want to see Bessie. But then, Mandy always wanted to see all of Animal Ark's patients.

James agreed enthusiastically to Mandy's plan.

'Great idea,' he said. 'I'll come round straight away.' He was nearly as keen as Mandy to see Bessie.

Mandy made her way to the residential unit. This was for animals who had to stay at Animal Ark while they were being looked after. Scrap had arrived only the day before and Mandy was determined to make the little kitten feel at home.

'Hello, Scrap,' she said, as she walked down the row of animal cages.

A black-and-white kitten looked up and limped to the side of the cage, pushing a paw through the bars. One of its legs was thickly bandaged and there was a dressing on its abdomen. In fact, there seemed to be more bandage than kitten.

'Poor Scrap,' said Mandy, opening the cage and taking the little animal out. 'Are you feeling sore? You'll soon be better, don't worry.'

Mandy was determined that she was going to be a vet too when she grew up. She spent every minute her parents would allow around the animals that came into Animal Ark. Scrap was her favourite at the moment. The little kitten had taken on a much bigger cat in a fight and lost.

Scrap had been in a sorry state when his owner brought him into Animal Ark. Even Simon, the practice nurse, had thought the kitten couldn't be saved. But Mrs Hope had spent two hours working on the little kitten's leg and abdominal injuries. He was getting on nicely now.

Mr Hope looked into the residential unit just as Mandy was putting Scrap back into his cage.

'Ready?' he asked.

Mandy nodded. 'I've cleaned the cage,' she replied. 'I'll just wash my hands.'

Mr Hope turned as the sound of a bicycle bell came floating through the open window.

'That sounds like James.'

Mandy turned off the tap and dried her hands on a paper towel. 'Ready!' she cried.

Two

'There it is,' said James, shoving his glasses up his nose and pointing to a spot on the Ordnance Survey map.

The Land-rover crested the hill above Welford and Mandy leaned over to look where James was pointing.

'Drysdale Farm,' she said. She took a hand-drawn map out of her project folder and scanned it. 'It should be just about here.' She put a cross in pencil on the map.

'That looks very professional,' commented Mr Hope from the front seat.

James looked pleased. 'It took us ages to draw

that map,' he said. 'We're putting all the farms and houses we're studying on it. They're all at least a hundred years old.'

Mr Hope turned the Land-rover on to a farm track. 'Drysdale is certainly old,' he said. 'It's been in Nick's family for generations. The Summers had always raised horses there. But by the time Nick took it on, the farm was falling to bits.'

'How come?' asked James.

Mr Hope shrugged. 'I don't know the whole story,' he admitted. 'There was a terrible fire at the farm about forty years ago and after that the whole place was abandoned. Then young Nick arrived about a year back and said he was going to start raising horses again.'

'It sounds as though that would be a really interesting story for our project,' James said thoughtfully.

Mandy's thoughts were elsewhere. 'What happened to the horses?' she asked.

'What horses?' her dad said.

'The ones that were there when the fire happened,' said Mandy.

Mr Hope smiled. 'Trust you, Mandy,' he said. 'You always think about the animals, don't you?'

'Of course,' said Mandy. 'Animals are *important*!'

'You could ask Grandad all about it,' Mr Hope said. 'He's bound to remember the fire.'

'Good idea!' said James.

Mr Hope drew the Land-rover to a stop in the farmyard. Mandy looked around. It was obvious somebody had been working very hard. There were bags of cement propped up against the stable wall and a half-built structure on the other side of the stableyard.

'That must be the new stable block,' Mandy said. 'I wonder how many horses Nick is planning to have.'

'Here he is now,' Mr Hope said. 'You can ask him all the questions you like – after we've had a look at Bessie.'

A young man came out of the stable block to welcome them.

Nick Summers was in his mid-twenties. He was tall and thin with wavy dark hair and deep-blue eyes. At the moment his eyes looked worried and his face was drawn with tiredness.

'It was good of you to come, Adam,' he said to Mr Hope. 'Bessie seems to be getting more restless all the time. I've been up most of the night with her. She's pawing the ground a lot.'

'It might just be discomfort,' Mr Hope said. 'It can't be easy carrying two foals.'

'I hope so,' said Nick. 'She should have another three weeks to go.'

'I hope you don't mind a couple of visitors,' Adam Hope said. 'When Mandy heard I was coming to visit Bessie, I couldn't keep her away.'

Nick smiled and his whole face lit up. 'Bessie will be delighted to see you, Mandy,' he said. Nick had already discovered that Mandy loved *all* animals.

'This is James,' Mandy said as they walked towards the stable block. 'We're doing a project about old farms and stuff in the area. Do you think we could ask you some questions about Drysdale? It's so old, you see, it'll be great for our project.'

Nick laughed and ran a hand through his mop of curly hair. 'Drysdale is certainly old enough,' he said. 'Just look at these stables. If I don't get a move on they're going to fall apart before Bessie's twins are even born.'

Mandy looked across the stableyard to the half-finished building. 'Are those the new stables?' she asked.

Nick nodded. 'They were supposed to be finished by now,' he said as they passed through the door of the old stables. 'I hadn't realised just how much work it would be.'

'You're doing a great job, Nick,' Mr Hope said. 'You're working sixteen hours a day from what I hear.'

Nick looked around the old-fashioned stalls. 'It still isn't enough,' he said. 'This place isn't safe any longer. I just hope we don't have any really bad weather before I get the new ones finished. These leak like a sieve as it is.'

'You'll manage it, Nick,' Mr Hope said. 'But it is a huge amount of work for one person to take on.'

'Who said anything about one person?' said a voice from the far end of the stables. 'I've heaved so many bricks and shovelled so much cement, I could get a job on a building site any day.'

Mandy grinned as a young woman in jeans, gumboots and a tatty old jersey poked her head out of the end stall. It was Fiona Armour, Nick's girlfriend.

'You'd never think Fiona was Mrs Ponsonby's niece, would you?' whispered James, grinning.

Mandy smiled as she thought of Mrs Ponsonby

with her big flowery hats and high-heeled shoes. She was certainly nothing like Fiona.

'Hi, Fiona!' she said.

'Come and see Bessie,' Fiona replied.

Fiona had a round, rosy face and soft brown hair tied up on top of her head in an untidy knot.

Mandy and James ran towards the stall. 'Hello, Bessie,' Mandy said softly.

The big black mare turned her head at the

sound of Mandy's voice and whickered softly. Mandy stretched up a hand and stroked her neck. The mare moved restlessly from side to side.

'How is she?' asked James.

Fiona ran a hand through her hair making it even more untidy. 'She's getting a bit tired,' the girl said. 'This is hard work for an old lady like Bessie.'

'I hope her foals are black just like their mum,' Mandy said. 'Bessie's coat is so shiny.'

'I don't mind what colour they are so long as they're healthy,' Nick said as he and Mr Hope arrived at the stall.

'Of course, that's the most important thing,' Mandy said.

Mr Hope ran a hand over Bessie's flank.

'Why don't we go and have a cool drink while your dad is examining Bessie?' Fiona said to Mandy and James. 'And maybe some cherry cake.'

James nodded eagerly. 'That sounds great. I'm starving,' he said.

'You're *always* starving,' laughed Mandy.

They left Mr Hope in the stables with Nick and Bessie and walked across the stableyard to the house.

'Fiona,' Mandy said. 'Can we ask you some questions about Drysdale Farm?'

Fiona shrugged. 'Ask me anything you like,' she said. 'But I don't know if I can be any help. What do you want to know?'

James explained about the local history project while Fiona poured them all glasses of juice and cut up a delicious-looking cherry cake.

'I don't know too much about the history of the place,' Fiona said. 'Only that there was a fire here years ago and Nick's grandfather left the area and started a building business in York.'

'What about Nick's father?' asked Mandy. 'Didn't he ever want to come back to Drysdale?'

Fiona frowned. 'I don't think so,' she said. 'He was dead against Nick trying to restart the farm.'

'Why?' said James, biting into the cherry cake.

Fiona shook her head. 'Search me,' she said. 'Nick doesn't talk about it much. All I know is that Nick's dad made a bargain with him. Nick did a building course and in return his dad said he could have a year to see if he could make a go of the farm.'

'A year?' said Mandy. 'But Nick has been here a year already.'

'Not quite a year yet,' said Fiona. 'He still has a few more weeks to go.'

'And what happens if he doesn't make a go of it by then?' James asked.

Fiona's eyes darkened. 'If he can't prove to his father that it's a success then Mr Summers is going to sell the farm and Nick will have to go into the family business in York. That was the agreement.'

'But Mr Summers can't do that!' said Mandy.

Fiona frowned. 'Oh yes he can,' she said. 'The farm doesn't belong to Nick. It belongs to his father. Mr Summers can do what he likes with it. He's already shown someone round.'

'But Mandy's dad says the Summers family have been here for hundreds of years,' said James. 'They're part of local history.'

'And their horses,' added Mandy. 'You mean there won't be horses at Drysdale any more? Doesn't Mr Summers *like* horses?'

Fiona sighed. 'I don't know,' she said. 'I think it's got something to do with that fire years and years ago. If you ask me there's something behind all this.'

'But Nick *will* make a success of Drysdale,' James said.

'I hope so,' said Fiona. 'If only to show Aunt Amelia that she isn't always right.'

'Mrs Ponsonby?' said James. 'Why doesn't she want Nick to succeed?'

Fiona grinned. 'I've asked her that a hundred times,' she said. 'And all she says is she can't bear to see me going around in filthy old jeans and gumboots.'

'That's ridiculous,' said Mandy. 'As if the horses care what you're wearing!'

'Well said, Mandy,' Fiona replied, giggling. 'I must try that one on Aunt Amelia next time she complains about my clothes. She'll probably explode!'

Mandy looked out of the farm kitchen window. The old stable block really *was* falling to bits and the new one was only half finished. The farmhouse itself was in a terrible state with peeling paint and slates missing from the roof.

As she watched, Mr Hope and Nick came out of the stable block.

'Here come Nick and Dad,' Mandy said. 'Nick looks as if he could do with a cup of tea.'

Fiona shook her head. 'He won't stop for a break,' she said. 'He even eats his lunchtime sandwiches while he's working.'

Mandy saw Nick say goodbye to her father then walk across the yard to the bags of cement. He heaved one up on to his shoulders and disappeared into the new stable block. The next moment Mandy heard the sound of a cement mixer starting up.

Mandy and James went out to meet Mr Hope.

'I'll just say goodbye to Nick,' Mandy said, dashing off towards the new stable block.

The sound of the cement mixer masked her footsteps and Nick didn't hear her approach. Mandy peered into the new stable block. Nick was shovelling cement powder into the mixer. Sweat ran down his forehead and, as he lifted a hand to brush it away, Mandy saw that his face was strained and pale. He didn't look his usual smiling self. He looked exhausted. No wonder! He had been up all night with Bessie and now he had all this heavy building work to do.

Mandy bit her lip and slipped away without saying goodbye. Somehow she didn't want to waste *any* of Nick's time. How long did he have? A few weeks. And no doubt he was worried about Bessie. If the foals weren't all right it would be the final blow. Nick would have to give up Drysdale Farm.

Three

Mandy and James ran into Mrs Ponsonby that evening at Welford church. They wanted to get some material about the building for their project and they had taken Blackie along for a walk.

'Of course if you're looking for local history you should do a piece on Bleakfell Hall,' Mrs Ponsonby said as she arranged a huge vase of flowers in the church porch.

'Mrs Ponsonby should just wear a vase on her head,' James whispered to Mandy. 'Nobody would notice the difference.'

Mandy giggled. Mrs Ponsonby always wore the

most amazing hats. The one she was wearing now was bright pink and covered in artificial flowers.

'What was that, James?' asked Mrs Ponsonby. 'Don't mumble.'

'We thought we would get some photographs of the church,' James said quickly. 'It's more than two hundred years old.'

Blackie's ears pricked up as there was a sound at the church door. Two men came into the porch. It was Mandy's grandad and his friend, Walter Pickard.

'The church is a lot older than that,' Grandad said.

Blackie and Mrs Ponsonby's dog, Pandora, raced over to him, barking a welcome.

'Hi, Grandad. Hello, Mr Pickard,' Mandy said. 'Have you come for bell-ringing practice?'

Grandad nodded. He and Walter Pickard were bellringers at the church. Mandy loved to hear them practising.

Pandora barked and tried to climb up Grandad's leg. Walter Pickard scooped up the little dog.

'Hello there, little miss,' he said. 'Where's your chum?'

Mrs Ponsonby turned quickly and set the vase of flowers rocking. Mandy made a dive and caught it just in time, steadying it.

'Toby!' Mrs Ponsonby shrieked. 'Where are you?'

There was a scampering sound and a scruffy little mongrel shot out of the church and into the porch.

'Naughty boy,' scolded Mrs Ponsonby. 'Why are you always running off?'

Mrs Ponsonby had adopted Toby when the little dog had been abandoned but she had never managed to make him behave.

'He's probably chasing mice,' said Grandad.

Mrs Ponsonby drew herself up. 'Mice!' she exclaimed.

Blackie's ears pricked up and he and Toby raced off out of the porch door and into the churchyard.

'In an old place like this there are bound to be mice,' James said.

'Just because a building is old doesn't mean there have to be mice,' said Mrs Ponsonby. 'Bleakfell is very old and I assure you there are no mice in *my* house.' Mandy grinned. Bleakfell Hall was the huge old mansion where Mrs

Ponsonby lived. The mice were probably too scared to set foot in Mrs Ponsonby's house, Mandy thought with a smile.

'How's your project going?' Grandad asked. 'I hear you've been up to Drysdale. How is young Nick getting on?'

'He's working really hard,' Mandy said. 'Grandad, do you remember the fire at Drysdale?'

Grandad scratched his head. 'I certainly do,' he said. 'That was a terrible night. The fire started in one of the stable blocks and the whole place went up in flames. You could see the glow of it from the village.'

'Couldn't the fire brigade put it out?' asked James.

'They could have – *if* they'd got there in time,' said Walter Pickard. 'But the weather was dreadful. It was the middle of winter. The moor road was blocked with snow.'

'Some of us got through on tractors,' said Grandad. 'But by then most of the stables were destroyed and all we could do was try to get the horses to safety until the fire engines could get through.'

'Did you manage to save the horses?' said Mandy.

Grandad shook his head. 'Not all of them,' he said. 'The place was like an inferno. Smoke and flames everywhere. George Summers, Nick's father, was in a blind panic by the time we arrived. I had to drag him out of the stable block. He was badly burned as it was, trying to rescue the rest of the horses.'

'It took two of us to hold him back,' said Walter. 'He was all for going back in even though the whole place was alight. He'd have been killed for sure. It was madness even to think of going back in there.'

'George always was pig-headed,' said Mrs Ponsonby. 'But I never saw him so upset as he was after that fire. Then the family moved away.'

'It was devastating,' said Grandad. 'It changed a whole way of life for the Summers. Their family had always raised horses at Drysdale. Still, now young Nick is back. I never thought I'd see the day when Drysdale was a horse farm again. I wish him all the luck in the world. Everybody in the village that remembers that fire wishes Nick luck.'

'Hmmph!' said Mrs Ponsonby. 'That boy will never make a go of Drysdale but there's no telling him. He's stubborn – just like his father!'

'Did you know Mr Summers well?' Mandy asked, interested.

Mrs Ponsonby jammed the last few flowers into the vase and scooped Pandora out of Walter's arms and into her own. 'I was at school with him when we were children,' she said.

James's eyes widened and his glasses slid right down his nose.

'Children?' he said in disbelief.

Mrs Ponsonby looked down her nose at him. 'Even *I* was a child once, James Hunter,' she said.

Grandad put a hand over his mouth and Walter Pickard started coughing. Mandy bit her lip. She couldn't imagine Mrs Ponsonby as a child. She had a sudden vision of a miniature Mrs Ponsonby – complete with flowery hat.

'George Summers was all right,' Grandad said.

'Stubborn!' Mrs Ponsonby repeated. 'Just like Nick. I've told Fiona he's wasting his time with that farm but she won't listen either. Young people today think they know everything. Come along, Toby! Where on earth have you got to *now*?'

And with that, Mrs Ponsonby swept out of the

church porch with Pandora in her arms.

'Wow!' said James. 'Poor Fiona!'

'And poor Nick,' said Mandy. She turned to her grandad to ask more questions about Nick's father but she didn't get the chance.

'That reminds me,' Grandad said. 'I stopped in at Animal Ark on the way down. Jean said Nick had just phoned to ask your dad to go up to Drysdale after surgery. I think Bessie is ready to give birth.'

Mandy looked at her grandad in horror. 'But it's too soon,' she cried. 'The foals aren't due yet!'

Grandad looked concerned. 'I'm only telling you what Jean said,' he replied.

Mandy frowned. Jean Knox was the receptionist at Animal Ark. She wouldn't get a message like that wrong. Mandy turned to James.

'James, do you mind taking the photographs on your own? I want to get home and see what's happening.'

James nodded. 'No problem.'

Mandy raced out of the church porch and leapt on to her bike. Mr Summers, the project and the photographs were all forgotten. When an animal was in trouble Mandy could think of nothing else!

The Land-rover was just turning out of the drive at Animal Ark when Mandy arrived home. She slewed her bike to a stop and ran towards it. Mr Hope stopped the Land-rover and leaned out of the window.

'Grandad told me the foals are being born,' Mandy said breathlessly.

Adam Hope looked at her flushed face. 'Jump in,' he said. 'You can ring Mum from the car and let her know where you've gone. Hurry, Mandy!'

Mandy wrenched open the Land-rover door and scrambled in. Her dad's face looked very serious.

'I've just had another call from Nick,' he said. 'Things aren't looking too good. You'll have to stay out of the way unless I need your help. This is an emergency. I only hope I'm in time to do a caesarian section.'

'You mean cut the foals out of Bessie's tummy?' Mandy asked.

Mr Hope smiled. 'It sounds a lot worse than it is,' he said. 'It isn't *that* big an incision and it'll be a lot safer for Bessie than giving birth to two foals naturally. I just didn't expect the foals this soon.'

Mandy swallowed, unable to speak. Bessie's foals! They had to be all right. They just had to.

Mandy didn't speak all the way to Drysdale. Mr Hope was concentrating on his driving, going as fast as was safe. As they turned into the stableyard, she asked only one question.

'Is Fiona here?'

Adam Hope shook his head. 'She's at work in Walton. Nick is all on his own.'

They found Nick in the stables bent over Bessie, stroking her. He was speaking to the mare in a low voice, encouraging her, soothing her. Mandy stood for a moment and watched him.

The big mare was lying on her side in her stall. She was restless, stretching her neck, eyes rolling. As Mandy looked on, Bessie began to calm down, responding to Nick's voice and gentle hands. At last the mare lay back. Her neck and flanks were soaked in sweat but her eyes had stopped rolling and she seemed calmer.

Nick turned a worried face to them.

'She's doing her best,' he said. 'But I don't know if she's going to make it.'

Mandy heard his words but her eyes were on Bessie – and a tiny little foal lying on the straw beside her.

'Oh, she's had one,' she said.

'I think the other one is already in the birth canal,' said Nick. 'Bessie is trying to push.'

'Too late for a caesarian, then,' Mr Hope said. 'Bessie is going to have to do all the work herself.'

Mandy turned to him. 'Oh Dad, she will be OK, won't she?' She pleaded.

'I hope so, Mandy,' Adam Hope said.

He moved forward, running his hand over Bessie's neck. The mare bent and started licking the little foal. The foal lifted its head and tried to struggle to its feet on long, spindly legs. As Mandy watched, the little animal stood up shakily and almost immediately collapsed again.

Nick smiled in spite of his worry. 'This little fellow is going to be all right,' he said. 'It's the other one I'm worried about. I don't know if Bessie has enough strength left to give birth to it.'

Adam Hope was getting into his long green

overall. Mandy looked at the mare. Bessie's mane was soaked with sweat and she was trembling.

'Poor Bessie,' said Mandy. 'Isn't there anything I can do to help?'

Mr Hope looked at her. 'Yes, there is,' he decided, pulling on his rubber gloves. 'Come with me, Mandy. And bring that blanket.'

He scooped the little foal gently into his arms. Mandy pulled an old blanket down from the stable door and looked at Nick. 'It'll be all right,' she said. 'Dad will take care of Bessie and her foals.'

Nick nodded. 'I hope so,' he replied.

Mandy followed her dad into the next stall. Mr Hope laid the little foal down on a pile of fresh straw.

'Now, listen carefully, Mandy,' he said. 'When foals are born their mothers lick them to stimulate their system so that they can stand. Usually it happens quite quickly but Bessie can't manage, not with another foal to give birth to.'

'What do you want me to do?' Mandy asked.

Mr Hope smiled at her. 'Take Bessie's place,' he said. 'Rub this little one with the blanket to dry him off and start his circulation moving.

With any luck he'll be able to stand on his own in half an hour or so. OK?'

Mandy swallowed. 'OK,' she said.

'I'll be right next door if you need me,' her dad said. 'Just try to get him up on his feet.'

Mandy watched as her dad hurried from the stall then she turned to the foal. His forelegs scrabbled at the straw but, every time he got a grip, one of them would give way.

'Come on, little fellow,' Mandy said softly. 'I might not be as good as Bessie but I'll do my best.'

She took the blanket and spread it over the foal, rubbing gently but firmly. She could feel the heat of the foal's body under the blanket. As she rubbed, she felt the foal move beneath her hands. It was as if ripples of energy were coursing through his body. Mandy laid a hand on his head and he turned, lifting his head to look at her.

'You're so beautiful,' Mandy said, looking into the big dark eyes. She laughed. 'And you're black – just like your mum.'

The little foal whinnied very softly and lurched, bringing his forelegs up. Mandy gasped at the sudden burst of energy. The blanket slid from his flanks as he struggled to stand. First one front hoof, then the other. The blanket slid right off his back and on to the straw.

Mandy sat back on her heels, fascinated, as the foal's two back hooves tried to get a grip. Then, as if by magic, he started to stand, wobbling. His front legs gave way and he fell.

Mandy held her breath. But the foal hadn't hurt himself. Almost at once he was trying again, struggling to stand.

'You're so brave,' Mandy said admiringly. 'Come on, you can do it!'

The foal's head turned and he looked at her again. Mandy put a hand on his neck. It was warm and soft.

'Come on, little one,' she whispered, rubbing the blanket over his flank.

It was as if the foal had exploded into life. His front hooves flailed and he was half up. Then his back legs uncurled and straightened and he was standing – very unsteadily, but he was standing. He took a couple of tottering steps and his back legs gave way but this time he didn't fall. Instead, he lifted his head and scrabbled until he got another grip with his back hooves.

Mandy sat back. The foal was on his own now. He was learning to stand, trying to walk. He was going to be all right.

Mandy was so absorbed in watching the foal that she barely noticed when her dad came to stand beside her.

'Well done,' he said. 'Bessie couldn't have done better herself.'

Mandy looked up at him, her eyes shining.

'Isn't it the most wonderful thing you ever saw?' she said.

'I think *that* every time it happens,' Adam Hope said. 'It's what makes the job so worthwhile.'

Mandy's eyes opened wide. 'But what about the other foal?' she asked.

Adam Hope smiled. 'Bessie is pretty tired,' he said. 'But she's going to be fine after a good rest and a feed. The foal is born.'

Mandy felt her heart sink. Her dad hadn't said the foal was all right.

'Is it OK?' she said.

Mr Hope shook his head. 'Not really,' he said. 'The poor little thing is very weak.'

Mandy swallowed. 'But it's alive?' she said.

Mr Hope smiled. 'It's a she and, yes, she's alive, but she hasn't got much energy. Don't get your hopes up, Mandy. It's early days yet.'

Mandy looked at her father. She knew he would do his very best for the little foal, but things didn't sound too good. 'Can I see her?' Mandy asked.

Mr Hope nodded. 'Be very quiet,' he said. 'You won't find her as lively as this little one.'

Mandy looked at the foal. 'I'm going to see

your sister,' she explained. 'I'll say hello for you, shall I?'

The foal lifted his head. It seemed far too big for his spindly body. He took a few tottering steps towards her and then crumpled on to the straw.

'I can't believe he won't hurt himself doing that,' Mandy said, concerned.

Mr Hope laughed. 'Don't worry about him,' he said. 'He's doing fine. He'll get the hang of walking pretty soon. You'll see.'

Mandy giggled. 'It must be quite difficult to manage four legs all at once,' she said.

'I suppose it must,' said Mr Hope. 'I'll just check him over properly. Nick is next door with Bessie and the other foal.'

Mandy tiptoed into Bessie's stall. It was dim and warm. Nick looked up. He was kneeling beside a small black shape covered with a blanket. He smiled and his face was transformed; the exhaustion disappeared as if by magic.

'She did it,' he said, laying a gentle hand on Bessie's neck. 'I'm so proud of her.'

Mandy felt herself smiling back in spite of her worries about the foals.

'Well done, Bessie,' she whispered. 'And well done, Nick.'

Nick shook his head. 'Your dad was terrific,' he said. 'I was really worried. Come and see the other foal.'

Bessie whickered as Mandy came in and Mandy rubbed her hand over the mare's neck.

'Good girl,' she said softly. 'How *is* the foal?'

Nick's eyes were shadowed with tiredness again as he drew the blanket back. Mandy looked at the foal.

'She's black, like her brother,' Mandy said.

The foal's eyes were closed. She hardly seemed to be breathing.

'She's very weak,' Nick said. 'If she survives it'll be a bit of a miracle – and it'll take a lot of work to get her well. Your dad says she'll need extra feeding. Bessie won't have enough milk for both and the stronger foal will always get most of what's going.'

'You can feed her by bottle, can't you?' she said.

Nick nodded. 'It's just time I'm short of,' he said. 'And sleep! But I'll work night and day to keep this little one alive after what Bessie's been through.'

Mandy was full of admiration for Nick. He was trying so hard to make a go of things and he had so much to do.

'You really love horses, don't you?' she said.

Nick looked surprised. 'They're my life,' he said simply. 'All I want is the chance to raise them and look after them.' He looked at Bessie. 'She's been so brave. I'm sure this little foal will have just as much courage as her mother.'

'I can help with some of the chores around the stables,' Mandy said. 'And James would help too, I know he would. You'll need time to look after . . .' She hesitated. 'What are you going to call them?'

Nick smiled for the first time. 'I hadn't thought about it,' he said. 'What with it being an emergency, I haven't had time.'

Mandy thought for a moment. 'An emergency,' she said. 'Like Morse code. Why don't you call them Dot and Dash?'

'That sounds good,' said Nick. 'But which is which?'

Mandy thought of the little foal next door suddenly exploding with energy.

'I think the boy should be called Dash,' she said. 'He's got loads of energy. And this one is so tiny she isn't much bigger than a dot!'

'Dot and Dash it is then,' said Nick. 'And I'd be glad of your help, Mandy. Thanks a lot.'

Mandy looked at the tiny foal. She was such a little thing. 'Oh, I want to help you, Dot,' she said, her eyes brimming with tears. 'I really do want to.'

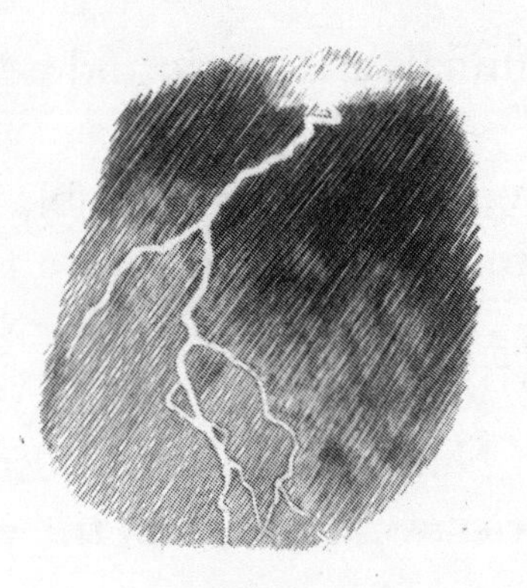

Four

'What next?' said Mandy two weeks later, pushing her hair off her flushed face.

Fiona smiled. 'You're a glutton for punishment, Mandy,' she said.

'What about Nick?' Mandy said. 'He was working on the new stable block when we arrived and he's still at it. He hasn't taken a break all morning.'

'*That*,' said Fiona, 'is a labour of love.'

'Just like Mandy,' James said, leaning on his rake. 'She doesn't mind how much work she does so long as she's around animals.'

Mandy looked round the stables. 'Particularly

when the animals are Bessie and her foals,' she said.

She glanced out of the open stable block doors and waved to Nick. He had almost finished the walls of the new stable block now.

'How is it going?' James yelled.

'Terrific!' Nick called back. 'Just one more course of brickwork to do and the walls will be done.'

'He's even promised to stop for lunch today,' Fiona said.

Mandy grinned. 'Things *must* be going well,' she replied.

'Thanks to you and James,' said Fiona.

Mandy and James had spent the morning mucking out the stables and laying fresh straw. They had started spending most of their free time at Drysdale and Mandy really enjoyed every minute of it – especially when Nick let her feed Dot. The smaller foal needed extra bottle-feeding and Mandy loved to hold the bottle while she sucked.

'Nick tells me Dot took some solid food yesterday,' Fiona said.

Mandy nodded. 'Just some grain from my hand,' she said. 'But it's a start.'

'It certainly is,' said Fiona. 'Dash is already on solid food and Nick was getting a bit worried about Dot.'

'She's still a lot smaller than Dash,' James said. 'But I expect she'll grow once she starts eating properly.'

'That reminds me,' said Fiona. 'How would you two like something to eat? You've been working non-stop for two hours now.'

James's eyes lit up behind his glasses. 'Sounds good to me,' he said. 'What about you, Blackie?'

The Labrador gave a short bark and wagged his tail.

'Blackie is just like you, James,' Mandy said. 'Always hungry.'

'There's nothing wrong with that,' said James.

'I'll just go and rustle up some lunch,' Fiona said.

'And *we'll* get the hay nets filled,' Mandy said firmly as James started to follow Fiona out of the stable.

'Oh, all right,' said James, coming back.

Mandy handed him a net. 'You know you love it too,' she said.

James nodded. 'It's great to help Nick out,'

he said. 'But it's even better to see how well Bessie and Dash are doing.'

Mandy frowned. Bessie and Dash *were* doing well. But little Dot still needed a lot of extra care and attention. She wasn't nearly as strong as her brother.

'But you are lovely, Dot,' Mandy said, leaning on the stall where Dot and Dash were. Dash looked up and whinnied. James stroked his mane and Bessie put her head over the loose box next door to see what was happening.

'It's all right, Bessie,' Mandy said. 'Dash just wants some attention.'

Bessie whickered and tossed her mane. Dot looked up at the sound and Mandy moved towards the little foal.

'You're looking better every day, Dot,' she whispered in the foal's ear. 'You'll soon be running around in the field. You wait and see.'

The foal looked at her with velvety eyes and Mandy felt a lump in her throat. Dot was certainly getting better but she still wasn't well enough to go out into the field with Dash. Mandy loved to watch Dash prancing about behind the stables. He seemed to fly on his spindly legs.

'Dot will soon be able to run about in the field with Dash,' James said.

Mandy smiled. 'How did you know that's what I was thinking?' she said.

James shrugged, embarrassed. 'I'm looking forward to it too,' he said.

Mandy took the hay net down from its peg and started stuffing it with fresh hay. 'Come on,' she said. 'Let's get this finished and then we can have something to eat.'

'Race you,' said James, thrusting hay into his own net.

They got the nets filled just as Nick put his head round the stable door.

'Food!' he said and Blackie leapt towards him.

'Have you finished the brickwork?' Mandy asked as Nick bent down to give Blackie a pat.

Nick nodded. 'I've just got the roof to put on now,' he said, then he shook his head. 'Did I say *just*?'

'You can do it,' said James.

'Maybe,' Nick said. 'With your help. I don't know what I'd have done without you two these last few weeks.'

'We'll be a little late reporting for duty tomorrow,' Mandy said. 'We've promised to go and see Mrs Ponsonby about our local history project. She wants us to put in a bit about Bleakfell Hall. She's got some old photos she says we'll be interested in.'

'We'd *much* rather be here,' said James as they walked out of the stables into the yard.

Mandy shivered. 'Oooh! It's cold,' she said. 'Where did that wind come from?'

'It said on the weather forecast this morning that there would be storms in some parts,' said James.

'Which parts?' Mandy said.

James shrugged. 'I didn't hear any more,' he said.

'Let's hope it isn't around here,' said Nick, looking at the tarpaulin he had rigged up over the new stable block. 'At least not yet. That cement has to set and I've got such a lot more to do. If we have a storm I'll have to stop work.'

Mandy looked up at the sky. There were huge grey clouds piled on the horizon and the wind really *was* getting up now. It blew her hair into her eyes and she shivered again.

'Let's get inside,' said James. 'I'm starving and it's cold out here.'

'Good idea,' said Nick.

They had almost finished lunch when Fiona looked up. 'It's getting awfully dark out there,' she said.

Mandy peered through the farmhouse window. There was a spatter of water against the panes. 'It's starting to rain,' she said.

'Oh, no!' Nick cried. 'I must get the cement covered up. That's all I need – rain!'

'We'll help,' said Mandy, jumping down from the table. 'Come on, James.'

'I'll come too,' said Fiona as Nick threw open the door. The wind whistled into the kitchen, blowing a newspaper on to the floor and whirling it across the stone flags. Nick caught the door before it crashed back against the wall. It took all his strength to shut it after them.

'Ow!' said James as they got outside. The wind was blowing hard now, driving the rain in front of it.

Nick looked towards the new stable block. 'Uh-oh!' he said. 'That tarpaulin is going to go in a minute. Come on, you lot.' He raced across the stableyard.

Mandy pelted after him. The big tarpaulin

covering the top of the stable block flapped in the wind. Nick reached it and made a grab for the end of the rope attached to one corner of the canvas, trying to tie it down. The wind whistled around Mandy's ears, whipping her hair into rats' tails as the rain fell even harder.

'Grab that rope at the other end, James!' Nick shouted, his voice almost blown away on the wind.

James made a dive for the rope but it flew out of his reach and caught Mandy a stinging blow across the forehead.

She hardly noticed as she flailed wildly, reaching for the rope. The wind buffeted her, almost knocking her off her feet. She stumbled and nearly fell. Then her hand grasped the rope. Another gust almost tore it out of her hand but she hung on grimly.

'Got it!' she shouted. 'You help Nick, James.'

The wind tugged at the rope. Mandy clenched both hands round it, ignoring the pain as the rough fibres scraped her palms. The wind was lifting the tarpaulin, getting in under it. Mandy twisted one arm round the rope. It sawed against the sleeve of her jumper.

'I can't hold it,' she yelled. 'The wind is too

strong. It's lifting the whole tarpaulin.'

Fiona raced over and grabbed the rope, hanging on with all her strength. Nick had managed to tie down one rope. Now he was working on another at the other end of the tarpaulin. He was struggling against the wind, trying to rope it down. His face was tight with concentration, his hair plastered against his head with the force of the rain. He wound his left arm round the rope and his face twisted in pain as the rope bit into his bare flesh.

James raced to help him and threw his whole weight on the rope. Nick unwound his arm from the rope, still keeping hold. Mandy gasped. The whole of Nick's forearm was scored deep red from the rope burn. Fighting against the wind and rain, he at last managed to fasten the tarpaulin down.

Mandy felt the rope she and Fiona were clinging to begin to slip.

'Hurry, Nick!' Fiona called.

'Coming,' Nick shouted back, plunging towards them. 'Hang on in there.'

There was an extra fierce gust of wind and Mandy heard a crash. She whirled round, rain stinging her cheeks, her hair over her eyes. The

rope tightened, threatening to crush her arm. She hardly noticed Nick arrive, taking the strain of the rope.

'Oh, no,' she gasped as the wind tore at her breath.

Fiona turned too. 'It's the old stables,' she shouted. 'Nick! Look!'

Nick looked up.

'No!' cried James. Then he too was running towards them.

Mandy's mouth hung open in horror. She could hardly believe her eyes. The roof of the old stables was starting to slip. It looked ready to collapse. It sagged as another gust of wind blew. Then the sky cracked open and lightning flashed across it.

'The horses!' Mandy cried.

'Leave the rope. Let it go!' Nick yelled. 'You can't hold it and there's no time to lose.'

Mandy opened her hands. The rope sprang free and whirled away on the wind. She looked down. Her hands were red and raw but she didn't have time to think about that now. They needed to save the horses.

Nick was already running towards the old stables. 'Stay here,' he yelled back at Mandy and

James. 'Do you hear me? Don't come near the stables.'

'But we can help,' said Mandy.

Nick's face was white, his hair streaming with rain, but his eyes were steady as he paused for a moment and looked at her.

'I'll get the horses out,' he said. 'Be ready to take them into the field – but don't come inside!'

Then he was off, racing alone for the stables.

The rain beat down. The tarpaulin flapped loose, waving wildly in the wind. Lightning split the sky. Suddenly, Mandy's hands began to hurt.

'Do as he says, Mandy,' Fiona shouted as she rushed past. 'It's too dangerous for you and James.'

Mandy looked at James. His glasses were streaming water. Another bolt of lightning seared the sky and thunder rolled.

'Your hands!' he cried.

Mandy glanced down. 'It doesn't matter,' she said. 'Come on. At least we can be ready to take the horses as they bring them out.'

'But what about this?' said James. The tarpaulin was flapping free all down one side. Mandy looked at the ropes that held it down on the other side. As she watched, an almighty gust of wind seized the canvas and one of the ropes snapped. The tarpaulin was hanging by one rope only, flying like a kite against the stormy sky.

'That's not important,' Mandy said firmly. 'We've got to save the animals, James. The horses are in danger.'

There was a shout from the old stable block and Mandy saw Nick struggling out of the building with Bessie. The mare was tossing her head, terrified by the storm. The stable block seemed to creak and sway. 'Get a cover, a cloth – anything,' Nick called. 'The foals are terrified. I can't get them out. I'll have to cover their eyes with something.'

Fiona rushed towards Nick and took Bessie's bridle from him. The frightened mare plunged as Fiona tried to lead her away. Mandy saw Fiona haul on the bridle, urging Bessie towards the field, away from the stables.

Lightning flashed again and Mandy watched in horror as an avalanche of slates crashed down into the stableyard from the old stable block roof.

'A cloth!' yelled Nick.

Mandy shook the rain out of her eyes. Where

was she going to find a cloth? Then she had an idea. 'Will this do?' she yelled over the wind as she tore off her jumper.

Nick grabbed it from her and plunged back into the building. The rain soaked through Mandy's T-shirt but she hardly noticed. Her heart lurched as another crack sounded. This time it wasn't thunder. It was the old stable block roof. A beam had snapped. More slates slid into the yard and the whole thing sagged even more.

Nick appeared, leading one of the foals. Mandy peered through the lashing rain, trying to see which one it was. Nick had Mandy's jumper over the foal's eyes. What it couldn't see wouldn't frighten it but the sound of thunder rolling in the distance made the foal tremble and start.

'It's Dash,' Nick said. 'Get him to the field. I'm going back in for Dot.'

James took hold of Dash's bridle and Nick raced back to the stable block.

Mandy grabbed James's arm. 'Look!' she said.

The whole roof was moving now, sliding inwards. Nick was in there – and he didn't have anything to cover Dot's eyes.

Mandy snatched the jumper. 'Take Dash to

the field,' she said to James. 'I'm going after Nick. He'll never get Dot out on his own.'

James made a dive for her but Dash plunged, his hooves clattering on the cobbles of the stableyard. James lurched sideways.

'Mandy!' he yelled. 'You can't go in there. You heard what Nick said.'

But Mandy didn't hear him above the roar of the wind, the pounding of the rain. She was flying towards the stables, plunging through the door. The sound of creaking timbers filled the stables as she searched for Nick. Outside the wind howled round the building, lightning flashed. In that moment's brightness, she saw Nick.

'Here!' she yelled, running towards him.

Nick grabbed the jumper and covered Dot's head. The little foal's eyes were rolling in terror.

'Get out!' Nick yelled to Mandy.

Mandy put a hand on Dot's bridle. 'Not without Dot,' she said.

Half-carrying, half-pushing the little foal, Nick and Mandy made their way towards the door. The roof timbers creaked and sagged. The whole building seemed to tremble on its foundations. Suddenly there was a dreadful crack.

Plaster and dust cascaded down, filling their mouths, their nostrils, stifling them. Mandy choked. Her eyes were gritty with dust and dirt.

'Quick,' croaked Nick, giving Mandy a shove. 'Out!'

Mandy almost fell through the stable door as Nick, with incredible strength, lifted the foal off its feet and charged through the door after her.

'Run!' Nick yelled.

Mandy ran, but not before she saw Nick urge Dot onwards. Once out of the creaking, dust-filled building Dot was much calmer but she was still shivering and her flanks streamed with water. Together Mandy, Nick and Dot hurried across the stableyard. Above them the sky split in two as lightning forked across it.

Behind them the roof of the old stable block finally gave way. It was as if it was happening in slow motion. The whole roof caved in on itself as it crashed to the ground in a shower of dust and dirt. Mandy's sob caught in her throat.

'Your stables,' she said.

Nick's face was streaked with dirt and rain. He passed a hand across his eyes as he looked at the ruin.

'They were done for anyway,' he said.

'No,' said Mandy. 'Your *new* stables. Look!'

Nick looked where she was pointing. The tarpaulin flapped against the half-finished building, great pools of water had formed on every surface, soaking the cement. Rain lashed the exposed beams.

'All your work,' Mandy said.

Nick drew in his breath. His eyes were strained and tired. But his hand stroked little Dot's flank.

'We got the horses out,' he said. 'That's the most important thing.'

'You can rebuild the stables,' Mandy said.

'I can try,' said Nick. 'But is it worth it?'

Mandy looked at him. He looked beaten and exhausted. His hair was thick with dirt and his arm streaked with blood from where the rope had bitten into it. His new stables looked as if they were ruined, but Nick's first thought was for the horses.

'It's worth it, Nick,' she said. 'You can't give up now.'

'I'll try, Mandy,' Nick said wearily. 'I'll keep on trying until the last minute. But don't be too disappointed if it doesn't work out.' He looked around at the devastation of all his dreams. The rain beat down. 'All I ever wanted

Five

'Nick *can't* give up, not now,' said Mandy as she and James parked their bikes outside Bleakfell Hall.

It was Sunday, the day after the storm, and Mandy and James were keeping their appointment with Mrs Ponsonby. Blackie had come too and was having a lovely time snuffling out all the interesting things under Mrs Ponsonby's laurel hedge.

'What else can he do?' said James. 'He's only got a week left.'

Many stopped, her hand half-raised to the big brass knocker on the front door. Both her hands were bandaged and riding her bike wasn't the easiest thing in the world but she kept telling herself that Nick was in a much worse state than she was.

'A week?' she said.

James nodded, his spectacles glinting in the sun. The breeze off the moors was soft and the sun was warm on Mandy's back. It was almost impossible to believe there had been such a fierce storm only the day before.

'If Nick can't get things sorted out by the end of this week, his father is going to sell the farm,' James went on. 'That was the bargain.'

Mandy looked shocked. 'But that's unfair,' she said. 'Nick's got so much to worry about already. Dot isn't well. He's really concerned about her. She's off her food again.'

Mandy's eyes darkened with concern as she remembered trying to coax the shivering little foal to eat while Nick rigged up a temporary shelter for the horses.

Dot had been wet through during the storm. That experience had set her recovery right back. Mandy had been so busy with Dot in the weeks before the storm that she hadn't realised how quickly time was passing. Now Nick's deadline was nearly upon them.

'We've got to do something, James,' Mandy said.

'What can *we* do?' asked James reasonably.

'I don't know,' said Mandy. 'But there must be something.' She crashed the door knocker down. It hurt her hand but it also made her feel better. The sound reverberated through the house but Mandy hardly heard it. Her mind was on Nick – and Dot.

'You don't have to knock the door down,' said a cheerful voice.

Mandy looked up. It was Fiona. Mandy smiled in spite of her worries. 'Sorry, Fiona,' she said, 'I was thinking about Nick.'

Fiona's smile vanished. 'He's just about given up,' she said. 'He'll never get the new stable block finished on time now. How are your hands? Were your parents furious?'

Mandy shook her head. 'They understood,' she said. 'They knew I was only trying to help Nick and the horses. Anyway, my hands are fine. Mum put some cream on them. She says they'll be better in a few days. What about Nick's arm?'

'He *says* it doesn't hurt,' said Fiona. 'You two are quite a pair.'

Mandy grinned. Fiona had the knack of making her feel better.

'There you are!' said a voice behind Fiona, and Mrs Ponsonby came into view with Pandora in her arms. Toby scampered forward and Blackie rushed to meet him.

'Amanda Hope,' Mrs Ponsonby said. 'Look at your poor hands. I've told Fiona I think Nick ought to be ashamed of himself, letting you injure yourself like that.'

'It wasn't Nick's fault,' Mandy said.

'That's a matter of opinion,' Mrs Ponsonby objected.

'Hello, Mrs Ponsonby,' James said quickly. 'We've come to look at the photographs for our project.'

'I've got them ready,' Mrs Ponsonby said, leading the way through the big dark hall to the sitting-room. 'Here we are.'

There were three big leather-bound books on the coffee table. Mandy picked up one of them.

'These are great,' she said, as she leafed through them.

James was chuckling over another book of photos. 'Look at the funny clothes people wore,' he said. 'And look at Bleakfell Hall. It looks just the same.'

Mrs Ponsonby settled down on a chair and began to describe the photos as Mandy and James went through the books. The last one was more modern than the other two.

'That's me,' said Mrs Ponsonby. 'That photograph was taken at the Welford Show when I was seven.'

James looked at the photograph. It showed a group of children standing in front of the village church. Mrs Ponsonby pointed to a tubby little girl with pigtails. James's mouth fell open. Mandy could tell what he was thinking: Mrs Ponsonby in pigtails!

But Mandy was more interested in another member of the group. 'Who's that?' she said, pointing to a boy seated on a black pony.

Mrs Ponsonby adjusted her glasses and peered. 'Oh, that's George Summers,' she said.

'You mean Nick's father?' Fiona said, looking at the picture.

Mrs Ponsonby nodded. 'I told you I was at school with him.'

'He's riding a pony,' said Mandy. 'I thought Nick's father didn't like horses.'

'Like them!' said Mrs Ponsonby. 'He was mad about horses.'

Mandy frowned. 'Of course. Grandad said they had to hold him back from trying to rescue those horses from the fire. But this doesn't make sense. If he liked horses enough to risk his life for them, why isn't he trying to help Nick?'

Mrs Ponsonby shrugged. 'All I know is that after the fire he moved away with his family and that's the last I ever saw of him.' She shook her head. 'He was a good deal older then. He must have been about twenty by that time but he hadn't changed. He was a stubborn little boy and he was a stubborn young man.'

'He must have changed,' Mandy said. 'Something must have changed him. You don't just suddenly stop liking horses for no reason.'

'Hmmph!' said Mrs Ponsonby. 'Pig-headed – just like his son. Nick looks just like he did when he was young – and he's just as mad about horses.'

Mandy shook her head. There was a mystery here that she just couldn't understand. Why had Mr Summers stopped liking horses?

'If you want copies of some of these for your project I can get them for you,' said Fiona. 'I'm going to York tomorrow. There's a place I know that can take copies from photos. They don't need negatives. It won't cost much.'

'That would be brilliant,' said James. 'Wouldn't it, Mandy?'

Mandy wasn't listening. 'York?' she said. 'That's where Mr Summers works, isn't it?'

Fiona nodded. 'The offices are in Barton Street,' she said. 'Why?'

'Oh, nothing,' said Mandy quickly. 'I was just wondering.'

James looked suspiciously at her and Mandy pored over the photos again. 'Which ones do we want, James?' she said. 'This one looks good, doesn't it?'

James was still looking at her a bit oddly but soon he too was busy choosing photos. Mandy's mind whirled with the idea that had come to her. It seemed that nobody could tell her what had made Mr Summers change his mind about horses or why he was so intent on selling the farm.

Well, she thought, one person *would* be able to tell her. Mr Summers!

Besides, it was high time somebody told him what a good job Nick was making of the farm. Mandy's mind was made up. She was going to York – and she knew how she was going to get there, if only James didn't let her down.

'What!' said James when they got outside. Blackie looked up and barked at the tone of James's voice.

'I tell you it's the only way,' said Mandy. 'Somebody has got to stand up to Mr Summers.'

'If you go to York with Fiona tomorrow you'll have to miss school,' he said. 'Your parents will never agree.'

'Then I won't tell them,' said Mandy.

James's glasses slid right down to the end of his nose and fell off. He bent and picked them up.

'Say that again,' he said.

Mandy bit her lip. 'Look, James, it's simple. I'll go out as usual in the morning just as if I'm going to school. You tell my teacher that I'm unwell. Tell her my hands are too sore to hold a pencil.'

'They aren't, are they?' said James, concerned.

'No,' said Mandy. 'But it's only half a lie so it'll make it easier for you to use that as an excuse. They are a *bit* sore and you aren't very good at telling lies.'

'And I'm not going to start practising,' James said firmly. 'It's not going to work, Mandy. You'll get found out and then we'll both be in trouble.'

'We won't get found out,' Mandy said. 'I'll be back before anybody has even missed me. It isn't as if I'm doing anything wrong.'

'Playing truant?' said James. 'You don't call that wrong? You can't skip school. Your mum and dad would go wild.'

'I told you, they won't know,' Mandy insisted. 'But I need your help.'

'No,' said James.

Mandy looked at him. He seemed quite determined. 'OK,' she said.

'You mean you'll give it up?' James said. 'I knew you'd see sense, Mandy. It's a daft idea.'

'Give it up?' said Mandy. 'Who said anything about giving it up? I'll just have to do it on my own. Only now I *will* get found out.'

James swallowed. 'You aren't serious?' he said.

Mandy nodded. 'Nick is running out of time, James,' she said. 'I just know there's something funny about Mr Summers turning against horses and he's the only one who can tell me what it is. I've got to find out why he's so set against Nick running Drysdale as a horse farm.'

James sighed. 'Oh, all right then,' he said. 'You win.'

'You mean you'll help me?' said Mandy.

James looked at her owlishly. 'Do I have a choice?' he asked.

Mandy smiled shakily. 'Not really,' she said. 'But, thanks, James. Now hang on a minute while I go back in and ask Fiona to give me a lift to York.'

'You aren't going to tell her you're going to see Mr Summers,' James said. 'She'd never agree.'

Mandy shook her head. 'No,' she said. 'I think I'd better say I want to go to the big library in York to do some research for the project. I'll tell her I've got permission.'

James shook his head. 'She won't believe you.'

'Why not?' said Mandy. 'I *will* go to the library as well as seeing Mr Summers. Why shouldn't she believe me? I don't tell lies.'

'You do now,' said James.

Mandy frowned. What James said was true but she had to see Mr Summers. She just had to.

'I won't be long,' she said. 'Wait for me.'

James nodded. 'Something tells me we're both going to get into a lot of trouble over this,' he said.

Six

'There's the library,' said Fiona, bringing the car to a stop. 'I'll pick you up here at twelve. Is that OK?'

Mandy nodded. 'Thanks, Fiona,' she said.

Fiona had been great about giving her a lift. She hadn't even asked any questions. Mandy thought she was too worried about Nick and the farm to be interested in Mandy's project.

'See you,' said Mandy as she hopped out of the car.

She watched Fiona drive off and took a street map from her pocket and looked for Barton Street. She felt like a criminal but she kept telling herself it was for a good cause.

'Three streets away,' she muttered to herself. 'I just hope Mr Summers is in his office.' She looked at the library as she passed. She really would try to go in and look up some information on Welford, she thought, as she made her way to Barton Street and stood in front of Mr Summers's offices. It would make the whole thing seem more honest.

Mandy looked up at the sign on the outside of the building. It said 'Summers and Son'. That would be Nick – only he didn't want to be part of the business. Mandy peered through the big glass doors. The offices were a lot grander than she had expected. There was a receptionist sitting behind a desk in the foyer. Mandy bit her lip. How on earth was she going to get past her?

The receptionist looked up from behind her desk and saw Mandy. Too late to escape now. Mandy pushed open the glass doors and walked inside.

'Yes?' the receptionist said suspiciously.

'I'd like to see Mr Summers,' Mandy said.

The receptionist hesitated. 'What about?' she asked.

'Drysdale Farm,' Mandy said before she could think up anything else.

'A farm?' said the receptionist. 'Are you sure you've come to the right place? Mr Summers's business is building, not farming.'

'But Drysdale is a very old building,' Mandy said. 'I'm doing this project about historical buildings . . .'

'Buildings?' the receptionist said. 'Why didn't you say so? Mr Summers is very interested in old buildings. He's always glad to be of help to students doing project work. Is he expecting you?'

Mandy shook her head.

'Mmm, that could be difficult,' said the receptionist. 'Just let me see if he's free. What's your name?'

Mandy told her. The receptionist spoke into the phone.

'Yes, Drysdale,' Mandy heard her say. 'Very well, Mr Summers.'

Mandy watched her put the phone down. The receptionist smiled. 'He says he'll see you now,' she said. 'Take the lift to the fifth floor. It's the door at the end of the corridor. Mr Summers will be waiting for you.'

Mandy smiled her thanks but she felt very far from confident as she went up in the lift to the fifth floor. She walked along the corridor to the door at the end. It was open and a man stood with his back to her, looking out of the window.

'Mr Summers?' Mandy said. 'I'm Mandy Hope. I'm from Welford.'

The man at the window turned. Mandy looked at his face. She couldn't believe this grey-haired, worried-looking man was the same person as the little boy with the pony in Mrs Ponsonby's photograph album. But that was a long time ago, she reminded herself.

Mr Summers moved forward. 'What can I do for you?' he asked. 'The receptionist said something about Drysdale.'

Mandy took a deep breath. 'It's about Nick,' she said.

Mr Summers's eyes narrowed. 'Nick?' he said. 'Is he all right? Has something happened?'

'Nothing's happened to *him*,' Mandy said, glad at least that Mr Summers was obviously concerned for Nick.

'What do you mean?' asked Mr Summers. 'What has happened exactly?'

Mandy took a deep breath. 'There was a storm,' she said. 'The new stable block Nick was building was damaged and the old one fell down. Nick has had to rig up a temporary shelter for the horses but Dot, the little foal, wasn't very well and now she's sick again. Nick is never going to get finished by next week. You've got to give him more time, Mr Summers, you've just got to.'

Mr Summers's eyes hardened. 'Did Nick send you to say this?' he asked.

Mandy shook her head. 'Oh, no,' she said. 'Nobody knows I'm here. At least, my friend James does, but nobody else. I tricked Fiona into giving me a lift because I thought if you knew how hard it was for Nick you wouldn't sell the farm. He loves it so much, Mr Summers. He's worked so hard and you should see him with the horses. He loves horses. You used to love horses too, didn't you?'

For a moment Mr Summers didn't say anything. Mandy held her breath. She saw his eyes go to a framed photograph on his desk. She couldn't see what it was. It was turned away from her. Then Mr Summers looked up at her.

'Nick and I have an agreement,' he said,

ignoring her last remark. 'I'll give him his year but I've already got some people called Marr who are interested in buying the farm. They've had a look round and think it would be ideal for turning into holiday homes.'

'Holiday homes!' said Mandy, outraged. 'But Nick will turn it into a working farm. It *should* be a working farm.'

'I've stuck by my side of the bargain,' Mr Summers said. 'I've given Nick a year. He has to stick to his.'

'But the storm wasn't his fault,' Mandy said. 'You don't know how hard he and Fiona have worked. They want to get married and live at Drysdale. It's going to be a horse farm again – if you give them more time.'

'Nick is a dreamer,' Mr Summers said. 'And Fiona is just as bad. She's just as impractical as he is.'

Mandy moved forward. 'No, she isn't,' she protested. 'Fiona is working really hard too. She's very practical and Nick really can make his dream come true.'

'So Fiona is practical, is she?' Mr Summers said. 'I suppose you think it's practical to bring you to York to plead for Nick like this?'

'She didn't know I was coming here,' Mandy said. 'I told you, I tricked her.'

'Then she isn't very clever, is she?' said Mr Summers. 'Not if she can be tricked by someone your age.'

'I might be young,' said Mandy, 'but I know what's right.'

'So telling lies is right, is it?' said Mr Summers.

Mandy felt tears in her eyes.

'Do your parents know you're here?' said Mr Summers.

Mandy shook her head dumbly.

'Then they soon will,' said Mr Summers.

'Hope?' he said. 'Isn't that the vet in Welford?'

Mandy nodded, biting her lip to stop herself crying.

Mr Summers reached for the telephone and Mandy heard him ask for Animal Ark. A few moments later she heard her father's voice. It sounded shocked. Then Mr Summers handed the telephone to her.

'Your father wants to speak to you,' he said.

Mandy took the receiver.

'Mandy!' said Adam Hope.

Mandy's breath caught in her throat. She had never heard her dad's voice so angry. She listened while he spoke to her. It wasn't pleasant.

'Stay right where you are,' he said. 'I'm coming to get you.'

'What about the surgery?' Mandy said. 'What about the animals?'

'You should have thought about that before you ran off to York,' Mr Hope said.

'But, Dad, Fiona can bring me back,' Mandy said.

'Fiona?' said Mr Hope.

Mandy explained then handed the receiver back to Mr Summers. She heard him and her dad making arrangements but she was too upset to listen. Her eyes went to the framed photograph on Mr Summer's desk. It was a photo of a young man and a foal. At first Mandy thought it was Nick. The boy looked about twenty or so. The foal was the image of Dash. Then she realised it wasn't Nick. The clothes were too old-fashioned. It was Mr Summers, his father.

Mr Summers put down the phone and saw her looking at the photo. He looked very sad for a moment.

'I had dreams once too, you know,' he said. Then he turned the photo face down on the desk. 'Come on. I'm taking you back to the library to meet Fiona. Your father wants to see you as soon as you get home. And *I'll* have something to say to Fiona about this business.'

Mandy turned and followed Mr Summers out of the room. Her dreams of helping Nick were shattered. She had failed. Mr Summers even had people lined up to buy Drysdale. Mandy had known Mr Summers intended to sell the farm if Nick didn't make a go of it but somehow it was different knowing there were already people wanting to buy it.

But even as she went down in the lift with Nick's father Mandy couldn't help wondering

Seven

'You're grounded for a week and that's an end to it,' Mr Hope declared.

Mandy gulped. She had never seen her father look so angry.

She opened her mouth to speak but Fiona laid a hand on her arm. 'Mandy has been so anxious to help us,' she said to Mr Hope. 'Her intentions were good.'

Mr Hope ran a hand through his hair. 'That's all very well,' he said. 'But she played truant, she told lies, she even fooled you, Fiona. I can't let that sort of behaviour go unchecked.'

Fiona looked at Mandy. 'I wish you'd been

honest about what you planned to do in York,' she said. 'I could have told you it wouldn't do any good.'

Mandy shook her head. 'I don't understand what Mr Summers has against Nick,' she said. 'He's trying so hard.'

Fiona smiled, though she didn't look very cheerful. 'I don't think he has anything against Nick. I think there's something we don't know.'

'There's altogether too much *I* don't know,' said Mr Hope.

Fiona turned to him. 'It was my fault,' she said. 'I should have checked with you that it was all right to give Mandy a lift to York.'

'You had other things on your mind, Fiona,' Mr Hope said. 'This was Mandy's fault – and James's.'

'James!' said Mandy. 'You can't blame him. I made him cover up for me.'

Mr Hope looked even more serious. 'Then you'll have to apologise to him,' he said. 'James has been grounded for a week as well.'

Mandy hung her head, miserable. Her plans had gone entirely wrong, she had got James and Fiona into trouble and now she couldn't even go up to Drysdale, just when Nick needed all the help he could get. She had made the whole situation worse.

'I feel so guilty about getting you into trouble,' Mandy said to James when she saw him at school.

'I knew what I was doing,' said James. He shoved his glasses up his nose. 'And I'd do it again, Mandy. I know it didn't work out, but it was worth a try.'

'But now you're grounded too,' said Mandy.

'Only until Friday,' James said. He smiled. 'It's Blackie I feel sorry for. He keeps trying to drag me out of the house. He can't understand why I'm not taking him for walks.'

'Poor Blackie,' said Mandy, feeling even more guilty. 'It's only a week,' James said. 'Cheer up!'

But Mandy found it really difficult to be cheerful. She kept thinking of Dot and the relapse the little foal had had after the storm. Mrs Hope knew how worried she was and kept her informed of Dot's progress. Even Mr Hope, though he was still angry with her, gave her a report whenever he had been up to Drysdale. But even though the outlook for Dot was brighter, Mandy didn't dare to believe her parents. She wanted to see for herself.

'Don't blame yourself so much, Mandy,' her mother said.

But Mandy *did* blame herself. By all accounts, Nick was working night and day, rebuilding the new stable block and nursing Dot. Mandy felt so useless. If only there was something she could do to help.

The only thing that got her through the week was looking after the animals at Animal Ark. If she couldn't help Nick by taking care of Dot, at least she could help her mum and dad by taking care of some of their patients.

She was cleaning out the cages in the residential unit on Friday when her mother came in.

'How is Scrap?' Mrs Hope said.

Mandy lifted the little kitten out of his cage and gave him a cuddle. 'He's being really brave,' she said. 'His leg must be quite painful.'

'Maybe he won't get into any more fights,' Emily Hope said, smiling. 'But I doubt it. He isn't called Scrap for nothing.'

Mandy tried to smile but it was difficult. Looking after the animals had helped but she couldn't stop thinking about Nick and the foals.

'You know, Mandy, you've been very good all

week,' her mother said. 'You haven't complained once.'

Mandy felt tears stinging her eyes. 'I've only got myself to blame,' she said. She looked at her mother. 'Is Dad still angry?'

Emily Hope put an arm round her. 'He was surprised more than anything else – and disappointed that you didn't tell us what you planned to do,' she said. 'But I've had a word with him and he knows you were only doing your best for Nick.'

'Thanks, Mum,' Mandy said. 'It's been really awful having Dad angry with me.'

'Cheer up,' said her mum. 'At least your hands are better now. Why don't you pop Scrap back in his cage and get your jacket?'

'What for?' said Mandy, surprised. 'I can't go out. I'm grounded, remember.'

'I got you remission for good conduct,' Emily Hope said. 'I'm going up to Drysdale to check on Dot. Why don't you come with me?'

'You mean it?' cried Mandy. 'Oh, thanks, Mum.'

'I'll give you five minutes,' said Emily Hope.

Mandy was outside and in the Land-rover in three minutes flat.

*

'There they are! In the field!' said Mandy, bouncing up and down on her seat.

'At least wait until I've stopped before jumping out,' her mother laughed, pulling up in the stableyard.

Mandy scrambled out of the Land-rover and raced across to the field. Dot and Dash were grazing with Bessie. As she ran over, the two foals lifted their heads and whinnied. Dash tossed his mane and cantered over to the fence on his long spindly legs. Mandy reached out a hand and stroked the foal's neck.

'Hello, Dash,' she said. 'I've missed you.'

Bessie and Dot trotted towards her and Mandy stretched out her other hand. Dot was still thin but she wasn't the shivering, terrified creature Mandy had seen last time she had been at Drysdale.

'Dot!' she said, as the foal nuzzled her hand. 'You look so much better.'

'Doesn't she just?' said a voice and Mandy turned to see Nick walking across the yard with Mrs Hope. 'She's started eating properly,' Nick went on. 'I'll say this for Dot, she doesn't give up easily.'

'She really *is* getting better,' Mandy said.

Nick nodded. 'She still likes to stay pretty close to Bessie,' he said. 'She isn't quite as adventurous as Dash. She isn't as strong as Dash either but she's getting there. I only wish I had a proper stable for her.'

'You've done quite well with that temporary shelter,' Mrs Hope said. 'I'll just take Dot across there and have a good look at her.'

Mandy looked around the stableyard while her mother unhitched the gate of the field and led Dot out. The new stable block was looking better than the last time she had seen it but it still didn't have a roof. Nick had rigged up a tarpaulin over one end of it so that the horses would have shelter. The old stable block was just a pile of debris now.

'I'll have to get that cleared away,' Nick said. 'There's just so much to do before I move out.'

Mandy whirled round and Dash shied at her movement. 'What?' said Mandy. 'What do mean, move out?'

Nick ran a hand through his hair and Mandy saw how exhausted he was. The rope burn on his arm was still noticeable.

'It's no good,' Nick admitted. 'I haven't even

got stabling for the horses. I've run out of time. I'll have to give up.'

'But you can't give up now,' argued Mandy. 'Not after all the work you've put in.'

'I can't do anything else,' said Nick. 'How can I ask Dad to back me when I don't even have a stable? I had to let those roof beams dry out after the storm. That's why I haven't been able to get the new roof on.'

'But you only need a roof on it,' said Mandy. 'You've got a stable block.'

Nick laughed a little shakily. 'Only!' he said. 'Mandy, face facts. I've failed. It's the end of the month. Dad is coming tomorrow. He's bringing some people down for a second look at the place. They're interested in converting Drysdale into holiday homes.'

'The Marrs,' Mandy said. 'He told me about them. But Drysdale isn't *meant* to be holiday homes. You can't let them do that to it. It's meant to be a working horse farm.'

'A working horse farm needs a stable block,' Nick said. 'One with a roof. I can't put a roof on the stable overnight, can I?'

Mandy looked at him. She had never seen Nick look so down – not even after the storm.

'But you'll lose your horses,' she said. 'You'll lose Bessie and Dot and Dash.'

Nick looked across the yard towards the field where Dash and Bessie were grazing. Suddenly Dash tossed his mane and raced across the field, hooves flying, mane streaming.

'It was just a dream,' Nick said. 'Dreams don't come true.'

Mandy stared at him. Grandad's words echoed in her mind: 'Everybody who remembers the fire wishes Nick well'. An idea was taking shape.

She looked at the timber frame of the stable roof. There was a pile of roof felting propped up against the stable wall and a load of wood stacked in the corner.

'Oh, yes they do,' she said. 'Dreams *can* come true. But sometimes they need a bit of help.'

'What?' said Nick.

'You've got all the materials for the roof,' Mandy said. 'What do you have to do?'

'Oh, just cover the beams with panels, felt it, nail it down, creosote it – nothing much,' said Nick bitterly. 'All I need is a few more days but tomorrow is the end of the month.'

'A few more days or a lot of help,' Mandy said.

Nick shook his head. 'Tomorrow is the deadline,' he reminded her. 'I don't have enough time.'

'You do if you get help,' said Mandy.

'I'll need an army,' said Nick.

'I'll get you an army,' Mandy said. 'I'll get you as many helpers as I can. We'll be here at seven tomorrow morning.'

'Where are you going to get an army?' Nick said. 'Forget it, Mandy. It's no use. I can't do it.'

'*You* can't,' said Mandy. 'Not on your own. But the village can do it.'

'The village?' asked Nick.

Mandy nodded furiously. 'Everybody knows what you're trying to do,' she said. 'Everybody is on your side. All you have to do is ask for help.'

'I can't ask strangers for help,' said Nick. 'I hardly know anybody in Welford.'

'You're a Summers, Nick,' Mandy said. 'You belong here. You aren't a stranger. And, anyway, I know everybody and I can ask them for help. You'll see, Nick. Seven o'clock tomorrow morning – you'll have your army. I promise!'

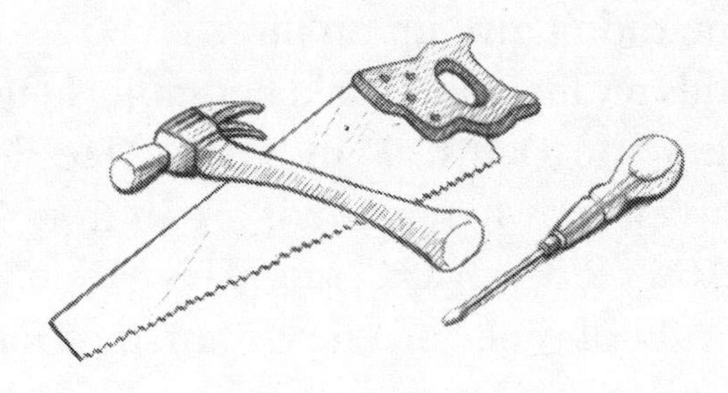

Eight

'This time, ask Dad,' Mrs Hope said as she drove back towards Welford.

Mandy heaved a sigh of relief. Her mum hadn't scoffed at her idea of getting the village to help Nick put the roof on the stable block.

'I will,' she said. 'Thanks, Mum.'

Emily Hope smiled. 'You never give up, do you?' she said.

Mandy grinned. She was feeling much better now that she had something positive to think about.

'Neither do you,' she replied. 'Look at Scrap. Even Simon thought he wouldn't pull through but you didn't give up on him.'

'So it's my fault, is it?' said her mum, laughing.

'Yours and Dad's,' Mandy said. 'He doesn't give up either when animals are in trouble.'

'Neither does Nick,' said Mrs Hope. 'He's spent a lot of time and energy nursing Dot back to health. She's coming on very well.'

'Is she going to get completely better?' asked Mandy.

Emily Hope nodded. 'She would be better off in a proper stable,' she said. 'She still has to build up her stamina. She isn't nearly as strong as Dash but in time she should be perfect.'

Mandy settled back and began to plan her campaign.

'Who are you going to ask to help?' her mum said, reading her thoughts.

'James first, of course,' said Mandy. 'And then – everybody.'

'How about Ernie Bell?' said her mum.

Mandy nodded. Ernie Bell lived in the row of cottages behind the Fox and Goose pub, not far from Walter Pickard. Ernie was retired now but he had been a carpenter. He would be *really* useful.

'Gran and Grandad will help,' Mandy said.

'And the McFarlanes from the Post Office and Mr Hapwell from Twycroft Farm and . . .'

'I know – everybody!' said her mum.

Mandy felt a bubble of excitement rising in her throat. She just hoped her dad would approve.

'Of course it's a good idea,' Adam Hope said when she told him. 'But I'm glad you cleared it with us first, Mandy.'

Mandy smiled happily. It was great to be back in her dad's good books.

'So, can I phone James?' she asked.

'Go ahead,' Mr Hope said. 'And you can tell Nick I'll be up there at seven with you. Mum is on morning surgery tomorrow.'

'Thanks, Dad,' said Mandy as she raced for the telephone.

'Brilliant!' said James when she told him her idea. 'I'll start phoning round too. Let's make a list and take half each.'

Mandy spent the next hour on the phone. She was almost at the end of her list when she heard a voice at the back door.

'What's all this about a gathering at Drysdale tomorrow morning?' said Mrs Ponsonby, sailing into the house. 'I've just been down at the village hall and your grandmother was putting up a notice, Mandy. She told me all about you going to see George Summers. That man always was stubborn. I hear you're playing him at his own game.'

Mandy put down the phone and turned to see Mrs Ponsonby, face red, hat askew, looking at her. It seemed she had been hurrying.

'I asked Gran to put up a notice,' said Mandy. 'Just in case I couldn't get round to phoning everybody this evening. There's a meeting of the village hall committee tonight so I thought the members could spread the word.'

Mrs Ponsonby looked down her nose at Mandy and straightened her hat. 'I suppose you were just about to phone me,' she said.

Mandy gulped. She hadn't actually thought of asking Mrs Ponsonby.

'Of course,' she said, crossing her fingers behind her back.

'And a good thing too,' declared Mrs Ponsonby. 'What this needs is somebody to organise it!'

'But I thought you didn't approve of what Nick is doing at Drysdale,' Mandy said.

Mrs Ponsonby drew herself up. 'Nonsense,' she said. 'I don't know where you got that idea. What I can't stand is people interfering. Do you know what George Summers said about Fiona? He said she wasn't practical.'

Mandy swallowed hard. Gran must have told Mrs Ponsonby the story.

'Not practical!' Mrs Ponsonby went on. 'As if a niece of mine wouldn't be practical. The cheek of it! We'll show him!'

Mandy tried hard not to smile. Good for Gran. If Mrs Ponsonby was on their side, Mr Summers didn't stand a chance.

'Now,' said Mrs Ponsonby. 'What's the plan of action? Organisation is what we need. And transport, of course. I'll organise that. I've already spoken to your grandmother about provisions. An army can't work without food, Mandy.'

Mandy nodded. She hadn't thought about that. Maybe Mrs Ponsonby would be a help after all!

Mandy, James and Mr Hope arrived at Drysdale just before seven on Saturday morning. The first thing Mandy saw was her gran and grandad's camper van and Mrs Ponsonby's car parked alongside it.

'Come along, Dorothy,' Mrs Ponsonby boomed, going over to the van.

Mandy's gran got out and followed, her eyes twinkling at Mandy.

Mandy rushed up to her. 'Thanks for getting Mrs Ponsonby to help,' she said.

Gran's eyes twinkled. 'It was easy once I told her what he'd said about Fiona,' she replied. '*And* I reminded her of how George Summers used to pull her pigtails at school.'

Mandy grinned. 'Gran, you're terrific,' she said.

'Dorothy!' Mrs Ponsonby shouted from the farmhouse door.

Nick sidled out behind Mrs Ponsonby and began to walk across the stableyard. He looked totally puzzled.

'Coming, Amelia,' Gran called back to Mrs Ponsonby. Then she winked at Mandy. 'Don't worry, I'll keep her busy in the kitchen. Good luck, Mandy.'

'Thanks, Gran,' Mandy said.

'Wow!' said James. 'Look at that. It *is* an army!'

Mandy whirled round as the sound of engines

filled the air. There was a long line of cars and vans snaking up the farm track from the road.

'They've come,' she said. 'They've all come!'

'What's all this?' said Nick.

Mandy looked at him. 'I told you I'd get you an army,' she said. 'Here it is.'

Nick looked stunned.

'Maybe you'd better get the horses into the field,' Mr Hope said. 'Something tells me the new stable block is going to be a bit crowded today.'

'I can't believe it,' said Nick. 'You mean all these people have turned out to help me?'

'That's right,' said James. 'They've come to put the roof on the stables.'

Mandy and James helped Nick lead Bessie and the foals into the field. Dash was eager to run around, kicking up his heels and racing across the grass. Mandy stood with an arm round Dot's neck. Bessie grazed quietly on Dot's other side. Little Dot was happier keeping close to her mother.

'You can do that,' Mandy whispered to her. 'You can run like Dash.'

Dot's ears pricked up as Dash cantered over to her and whinnied. The bigger foal turned away and moved off with dancing steps. He looked at Dot and whinnied again.

'Go on, Dot,' Mandy said. 'Go for a run, go and play with your brother.'

Bessie looked up and gave Dot a gentle nudge. Mandy slid her arm down Dot's flank and let it drop. Dot pawed the ground and took a few steps forward. At once, Dash whirled and started to race across the field. Dot's head came up and she began to canter forward. Then she too was running across the field, chasing her brother.

Mandy watched as the two black foals galloped over the grass, manes flying, tails floating on the wind.

'They look so beautiful,' she said.

Nick nodded. 'I never thought I'd see Dot do that,' he said. 'She's as brave as they come. First having to fight for her life when she was born and then struggling to survive after the storm.'

'You pulled her through,' Mandy said.

Nick shook his head. 'We all did,' he replied. 'You and James were a terrific help too.'

'And Dash,' James added. 'Dash is really fond of Dot.'

Mandy looked at the two foals frolicking in the field. Dash had slowed down, measuring his pace to his little sister's.

'And Dot would follow Dash anywhere,' Mandy said. 'Look at her! She's copying everything he does.'

Nick laughed. 'She'll have to build up her strength to do everything Dash does,' he said. 'Something tells me Dash is going to make a very fine jumper.'

'Really?' asked Mandy. 'That's wonderful. Oh, Nick, you're going to have the most famous stables in Yorkshire.'

'If we get the roof on,' said James, bringing Mandy back down to earth.

'Oh, cripes, I'd almost forgotten about that,' Mandy said. 'Look, Nick, everybody has arrived.'

Poor Nick still looked stunned but, as the cars and vans parked and people got out, he began to take it in.

'Where do you want us to start?' said Ernie Bell as he and Grandad and Walter Pickard came over to him. All the men were carrying bags of tools.

'We came prepared,' Walter said, smiling at Mandy.

'The panels,' Nick said. 'We've got to panel the beams first.'

'Right,' said Ernie Bell. 'Leave it to me. I'll get this lot organised.'

'Ernie knows what he's doing,' Grandad said to Nick.

Nick shook his head and laughed. 'Right at this moment, that's more than I do,' he said. 'I can't believe this is happening. Are you sure I'm not dreaming?'

'Not about all these people,' said Mandy. 'But your dream about the stables is going to come true.'

Nick looked at her. 'I think you might be right,

Mandy,' he said. 'And it'll be thanks to you if it does.'

Grandad laughed. 'Oh, don't think she's doing this for you, Nick,' he remarked. 'She's doing it for the horses.'

'That's fine by me,' Nick said. He looked at his watch. 'We've got twelve hours. Dad is due here at seven o'clock this evening – and he's bringing along some people who are keen on buying Drysdale. Unless we get the roof on and the place looking good by seven tonight Drysdale might well end up as holiday homes. We don't have a moment to lose!'

'Wow!' said James, collapsing on a pile of straw next to Mandy. 'I'm exhausted.'

Mandy pushed her hair off her flushed face. Mrs Ponsonby had called a halt for food. Everybody was sitting around with mugs of tea and huge plates of sandwiches.

'Look at Nick,' Mandy said. 'He looks really happy.'

'No wonder,' said James. 'The roof is almost finished. It's amazing.

' "Many hands make light work",' said Gran, coming round with a plate of home-made scones.

'Mmm,' Mandy agreed, taking a scone. 'This is great.'

'Can I have two?' said James.

'You can have as many as you like,' said Gran. 'You and Mandy need to keep up your strength for all the running about you're doing.'

James took another scone. 'We're only running errands and holding ladders,' he said.

'And unrolling felt and fetching tools,' added Mandy.

'And a hundred other things,' said Gran. 'You're saving the men a lot of leg work. If they had to run up and down those ladders all day long they'd never get finished in time.'

Mandy gazed at the new stable block. The panelling was on and all the felt nailed down.

'Do you think we'll finish in time?' she asked.

'We've got another three hours,' said Nick as he and Grandad came to fetch some scones. 'We should get it done. We've just got to creosote it now. We should just about make it.'

'The farmyard looks a bit messy,' Gran said, looking at the debris from the old stable block.

'That will have to wait,' said Nick. 'If we get the roof finished it'll be a miracle – and I'll settle for that. I'll move that debris into the field once

I've got the horses back in the stable. That way it won't be so noticeable.'

Mandy smiled, then her eyes narrowed in concern. 'Here's Fiona,' she said as the girl came running from the farmhouse.

Fiona rushed up, her face worried.

'What's wrong?' said Nick.

Fiona swallowed hard. 'Oh, Nick, that was Mr Hardy at the Fox and Goose. A man and a woman have just come into the pub for a snack.'

'So?' Nick was puzzled.

'They were asking the way to Drysdale,' Fiona said. 'Nick, it's Mr and Mrs Marr, the people your father was bringing down. They've arrived already. They're making their own way over – now!'

'But they can't be here yet!' cried Nick. 'It's only four o'clock. Dad said he wouldn't bring them over till seven.'

Fiona looked at her watch. 'It's almost five-thirty, Nick,' she said.

Nick's face went pale. He shook his wrist. 'My watch has stopped,' he said. 'The battery must have gone flat.'

Mandy's heart sank. 'But we've done so much. Surely we've done enough.'

Nick shook his head. 'The new stable block was part of the bargain,' he said. 'If I haven't got that finished the deal is off. It's no good. I've lost after all.'

'Your dad isn't here yet,' Fiona said. 'The Marrs are meeting him here. Surely it'll be OK if we get it finished by the time he arrives?'

'We still don't have enough time,' Nick said. 'Maybe if we had three hours. But now we only have just over an hour.'

Mandy turned to Fiona. 'What do they look like?' she asked. 'What kind of car are they driving?'

'Who?' said Fiona.

'The Marrs,' Mandy said. 'The people who want to buy Drysdale.'

'I don't know,' said Fiona. 'Why?'

Mandy started to run for the farmhouse. 'Because we've got to stop them,' she yelled over her shoulder. 'We can't give up. Not now!'

'Mandy, what are you up to now?' James shouted.

But Mandy had gone, almost knocking Mrs Ponsonby over as she dashed into the house.

Nine

'What on earth was that all about?' Mrs Ponsonby said, bustling up to them. She didn't wait for an answer. 'Dorothy, I've got to get back to Bleakfell to feed darling Pandora and Toby. They've been on their own all day, poor things. I'll come right back and help you clear up.'

Mandy's gran nodded but her face looked concerned. 'What is Mandy up to now?' she said to James.

James shrugged. 'We'll soon find out, I suppose,' he said.

'And we probably won't like it,' said Mrs Ponsonby.

They didn't have long to wait. Mrs Ponsonby was just getting into her car when Mandy raced out of the house again.

'Oh, Mrs Ponsonby, can you give James and me a lift to the Fox and Goose?' she called.

Mrs Ponsonby looked scandalised. 'The pub?' she said.

Mandy grabbed James and started dragging him towards Mrs Ponsonby's car. 'I phoned Mr Hardy,' she said to Nick. 'He's going to keep the Marrs there for as long as he can. I've told him to be very slow indeed serving up their meal.'

Nick looked bewildered. 'What good will that do?' he said. 'We need two hours at least to get the roof finished and the stables cleared up.'

'Don't worry,' said Mandy. 'I've got a plan. Just *hurry*, Nick.'

Nick stood watching them as Mandy bundled James into the back seat of Mrs Ponsonby's car and they set off.

'What plan?' said James, bewildered.

'*I'd* like to know what's going on too,' Mrs Ponsonby said.

Mandy sighed. There was nothing else for it. She didn't have any time to waste.

'The buyers have arrived at the Fox and Goose,' she said to Mrs Ponsonby. 'They're driving a dark-blue estate car. Mr Hardy is going to delay them as long as he can but that won't be long enough.'

'So what's the point in Mr Hardy doing it at all?' asked James.

'The point is that it'll give us time to get people organised,' Mandy said. 'I rang Susan Collins and she's ringing round a couple of other kids in the village to come and help us.'

Susan Collins was a schoolfriend of Mandy and James.

'Help us do what?' said James.

'To set up roadblocks,' Mandy said.

'*Roadblocks!*' James screeched.

'Maybe not roadblocks exactly,' Mandy said. 'I told her we need people on bikes stationed on every road out of the village. They've got orders to send the Marrs in the wrong direction; tell them roads are blocked because of the storm last week, tell them lanes are getting dug up – anything to stop them getting to Drysdale.'

James's mouth dropped open. 'Mandy Hope, I don't believe you're real,' he said. 'That's brilliant!'

'Hmmph!' said Mrs Ponsonby from the front seat.

Mandy's heart sank. She had forgotten about Mrs Ponsonby.

'I really can't approve of this, Amanda,' Mrs Ponsonby said.

Mandy bit her lip. Mrs Ponsonby was never easy to persuade – unless you could twist things round so that *she* got what she wanted. Mandy's eyes lit up.

'You don't want Mr Summers to sell Drysdale for *holiday houses*, do you, Mrs Ponsonby?' she said.

'Holiday houses!' cried Mrs Ponsonby and the car swerved. 'Certainly not. Nobody said anything to me about *holiday houses*. But I still cannot approve of what you're doing, Mandy. It sounds like vandalism to me.'

'It's to help Nick and Fiona,' Mandy pleaded.

Mrs Ponsonby thought for a moment. 'That young man has gone up in my estimation,' she said. 'And I must say, I've never seen Fiona look happier, even if I do disapprove of those dreadful jeans and gumboots.'

Mandy almost smiled. Trust Mrs Ponsonby to think jeans and gumboots were important at a time like this.

'So you'll help us?' said Mandy.

Mrs Ponsonby drew a sharp breath. 'Help you to break the law?' she said. 'I'm sure what you're planning must be against the law.'

Mandy's heart sank again.

'I think I shall pretend I didn't hear any of that, Mandy,' Mrs Ponsonby said. She nodded her head. 'Yes, that would be best. Just let's pretend my hearing isn't quite as good as it used to be.'

'That'll be the day,' James said under his breath.

'I heard *that*, James Hunter,' Mrs Ponsonby snapped but Mandy was almost sure she was smiling.

Mandy leaned across the front seat. 'Mrs Ponsonby, do you remember anything else about Mr Summers leaving Drysdale? I'm sure there's some kind of mystery there.'

Mrs Ponsonby pressed her lips together. 'I did hear that he was very upset when the farm caught on fire,' she said. 'Some of the horses were killed and others were injured. But I could never understand why he left. He was mad about horses.'

'I think he still is,' said Mandy. 'He's got a

picture of himself and a foal on his desk in his office.'

'Now that I come to think of it, his father, that's Nick's grandfather, was injured in the fire,' Mrs Ponsonby said. 'I think he was the one who wanted to leave. And he didn't think George could cope with the farm on his own – something like that. It was so long ago. And I'll tell you one thing, once a Summers has made up his mind there's no shifting him. Stubborn! Every one of them.'

'There's the Fox and Goose,' James said.

Mandy twisted round. A dark-blue estate car was parked outside.

'They're still here,' she said. 'Come on, James. Thanks for the lift, Mrs Ponsonby!'

Mandy and James tumbled out of the car and raced round to the back of the pub. Mr Hardy met them as they came in.

'They haven't gone yet,' he said, his eyes twinkling. 'It's funny. The oven doesn't seem to be working so well so they're having to wait quite a while for their meal.'

Mandy grinned. 'Thanks, Mr Hardy,' she said. 'Susan Collins will be here soon – and a couple of others. James and I are just going to get our bikes. Susan knows what to do. Can you keep the Marrs here till we get back?'

Mr Hardy winked. 'The coffee machine isn't looking too healthy either,' he said. 'I'll have to boil a kettle and you know how long that can take.'

Mandy and James tore out of the Fox and Goose and raced off in different directions to get their bikes.

'What's all the rush?' Jean Knox, the receptionist at Animal Ark, said as Mandy grabbed her bike from the back garden.

'I'll tell you later, Jean,' she said, leaping on to her bike. She stopped for a moment. 'Oh, Jean, if anybody comes asking the way to Drysdale, you don't know. OK?'

Jean's eyebrows shot up and her glasses fell off her nose and bounced on the end of their chain.

'It seems to me there's a lot I don't know,' she said. 'I hope you aren't up to more mischief.'

'It's in a good cause,' Mandy said, pedalling down the path.

'That's what you said last time and look what happened,' Jean called after her.

Mandy gave Jean a wave as she turned on to

the track that led to the village. Susan and the others would be at the pub by now. She just hoped Susan had got enough people.

James pedalled into the pub car park just as Mandy slid her bike to a stop. Susan *was* there, her ponytail bobbing about as she talked to another three of Mandy's schoolfriends. Mandy breathed a sigh of relief. Susan had rounded up Peter Foster, Andrew Pearson and Jill Redfern. Mandy had been at primary school with all three. They wouldn't let her down.

'I'll take the Walton road,' Susan was saying as Mandy and James hurried over to them. 'Peter, you take Church Lane. Jill and Andrew can take the moor road.' She turned. 'Hi, Mandy. Hi, James.'

'Susan, you're great,' Mandy said, smiling round everybody. 'Thanks a bundle, you lot.'

'That's OK,' Peter said. 'Andrew and I were only kicking a ball around in his back garden. This sounds much more fun.'

'But what exactly are we supposed to do?' asked Jill.

'Anything to delay the Marrs getting to Drysdale,' Mandy said.

'My bike could have a breakdown,' James said.

'Just don't do anything dangerous,' Mandy said. 'I've got a feeling we might be getting ourselves into more trouble.'

A face appeared at the pub window.

'It's Mr Hardy,' Susan said.

Mandy went over to the window as Mr Hardy opened it. 'I couldn't keep them any longer,' he said. 'They decided not to wait for coffee. I'm just making up the bill now – I'm a bit slow.'

'Right,' said Mandy, 'Thanks a million, Mr Hardy.'

She looked at her watch. Nearly six o'clock. They had to delay the Marrs for another hour and it was only a fifteen-minute drive to Drysdale.

'OK,' she said to Susan and the others. 'Good luck.'

The other five cycled off in different directions. Mandy parked her bike out of sight and waited. Five minutes later a man and woman came out of the pub.

'The service was so slow!' the woman said. 'I won't be recommending *that* pub to any of our visitors.'

The man nodded agreement as they got into

the car and set off. Mandy followed as fast as she could.

The dark-blue estate car was trundling up the main street when it slowed down. There was a boy lying in a heap at the side of the road nursing his knee and grimacing.

'Good for you, James,' Mandy said under her breath.

At first it looked as if the Marrs were going to drive past. Then James gave a yell and started to roll around. Mr Marr drew the car to a stop and Mrs Marr got out.

Mandy watched. James really was quite a good actor. It was a full ten minutes before he had to admit he was all right. And that was only because Mr Marr suggested calling an ambulance. Even Mandy wouldn't have wanted the Marrs to do that!

The next delay was at the crossroads of the moor road and the Walton road. There was a branch draped across the road sign, hiding the directions. Susan was leaning against the road sign. Mandy saw the car draw up and Mrs Marr lean out to speak to Susan. Susan pointed along the Walton road.

'Terrific,' Mandy thought as Susan waved and

cycled up the moor road to join Jill and Andrew.

Mandy waited. Another ten minutes and the car was back. This time Mandy pointed them back down the main street and told them to take the turning at Church Lane.

She looked at her watch. She couldn't really afford to hang about too much longer or the Marrs would get suspicious. This time when the car came past it didn't even stop but took the moor road. Mr Marr looked very bad-tempered indeed. Mandy frowned. The Marrs were on the right road now and they wouldn't trust Susan's directions again.

Mandy turned her bike to take the short cut behind the church. If she really hurried she might cut them off at the intersection.

Mandy's legs were sore from pedalling as she came out of the lane and on to the moor road. The Marrs' dark-blue car shot past. She had just missed them. But Mandy saw another car slowing down up ahead. Mandy recognised it: Mrs Ponsonby !

The Marrs' car drew to a halt. Mrs Ponsonby got out and turned towards the blue estate. Mr Marr leaned out of the window to speak to her and Mandy's heart sank. Mrs Ponsonby would point them straight to Drysdale. Then she realised Mr Marr was getting out of his car. She cycled on. Mrs Ponsonby's voice came loud and clear.

'It simply stopped and here am I in the middle of the road, blocking everything! Just as well this road gets hardly any traffic, isn't it? I do hope you aren't in a hurry. So kind of you to stop and help me.'

Mandy grinned. So much for Mrs Ponsonby not helping out! The Marrs had no choice but to stop. Mrs Ponsonby's car was stuck right in the middle of the road.

Mandy pushed her bike into a hedge and crept closer. She turned at the sound of bicycle wheels behind her.

'Hi,' said James, slowing to a stop. 'Susan and the others have gone off. They couldn't get beyond the Marrs on bikes so it was pointless trying.'

Mandy looked at her watch. 'We'll never keep them away from Drysdale for another half-hour,' she said. 'Not even Mrs Ponsonby can do that.'

'Mrs Ponsonby?' asked James, his glasses sliding down his nose.

'She's pretending she's broken down,' said Mandy.

'Wow!' exclaimed James as he pushed his bike into the hedge beside Mandy's. 'Let's get closer and see what's going on.'

Mr Marr had the bonnet up by this time and Mrs Ponsonby was smiling sweetly at him from the driving seat.

'Try it now,' said Mr Marr impatiently.

Mrs Ponsonby turned the key in the ignition and the engine coughed.

'Not a thing,' she said. 'Isn't it dreadful?'

Mandy and James hardly heard the big black car as it drew up behind them. It was very posh and very quiet.

'What's the trouble?' said a voice and Mandy whirled round.

'Mr Summers!' she said.

Mr Summers looked at her. 'You again,' he replied. Then his eyes went to the cars in front. Mrs Ponsonby was struggling out of the driving seat of her car.

'George Summers,' she said.

Mr Summers looked taken back. 'Amelia Ponsonby?' he said. 'What's going on here?'

'This lady's car has broken down,' said Mr

Marr. 'I was trying to help her. I must say, Summers, we've had the most terrible trouble finding Drysdale Farm. It seemed much easier when you brought us! This whole village seems to be full of children with no sense of direction, the pub was so slow we had to leave without coffee, and now this lady has had a breakdown right in the middle of the road.'

Mr Summers looked at Mrs Ponsonby and she smiled. 'Tut, tut,' she said. 'I never was any good with engines.'

'Nonsense, Amelia,' George said. 'I remember you fixed my motorbike for me once or twice.'

Mandy's eyes popped. *Motorbike*!

Mr Summers strode towards Mrs Ponsonby's car and reached in. He turned the key in the ignition and the engine roared into life.

'Well, fancy that!' said Mrs Ponsonby. 'You must have a magic touch, George.'

Mr Summers gave her a look. 'Amazing, isn't it?' he said. Then he turned his eyes on Mandy.

'I'm willing to bet you've seen this young lady a couple of times on your travels,' he said to the Marrs.

Mrs Marr peered at Mandy. 'Oh, yes,' she said. 'She's been behind us most of the way.'

Mr Summers frowned 'That's not all she's been behind,' he said. 'I suggest you get your car moving, Amelia, and let the Marrs past. We've got an appointment at Drysdale.'

Mandy's shoulders sagged as she watched the Marrs' car edge round Mrs Ponsonby and roar on up the moor road, closely followed by Mr Summers.

'Thanks for trying, Mrs Ponsonby,' she said.

'Hmmph!' said Mrs Ponsonby. 'George Summers hasn't changed. He always did think he knew best.' Then she opened the rear door of her car. 'Jump in then,' she said. 'You can leave your bikes here. We might as well see what happens up at Drysdale.'

Mandy and James got in but Mandy wasn't really sure she wanted to go to Drysdale. She chewed her lip in frustration. Had they done enough to delay the Marrs? Would Nick and the others have the new stable block finished? And, even if they did, would Mr Summers keep to his side of the bargain?

Ten

Mandy leaped out of the car as soon as it stopped. Mr Summers was just getting out of his own car and the Marrs were standing in the middle of the farmyard looking round.

The field gate was open and there were no horses there – only a pile of debris from the old stable block. Nick and the others must have moved it from the farmyard. But where were the horses?

Mandy looked at the new stable block. The stableyard was swept and tidy, except for the ruin of the old stables. Bessie was in a loose box and in the next box were Dot and Dash.

The stables were finished! Mandy examined the roof. The fresh creosote gleamed in the evening sunlight. Mandy thought she had never seen such a wonderful sight in her life.

'They've done it,' she said to James. 'They've finished the stable block.'

James grinned. 'Wow!' he exclaimed. 'I never thought they would do it in time.'

Nick came forward to meet his father. There was a streak of paint across his cheek and quite a lot in his hair but he looked happy.

Mr Summers glanced at his son, then he gazed around the yard and his eyes rested on the horses in the new stables.

'You did it?' he said in disbelief.

'Just,' said Nick, running a hand through his hair and getting even more paint in it. 'But I had a lot of help.'

Mandy looked at the villagers gathered behind Nick. Every one of them was smiling.

'It looks like you had the whole village helping you,' Mr Summers said. He looked round at Mandy and James. 'Including these two.'

Walter Pickard stepped forward. 'It's good to see you again, George,' he said. 'That's a fine boy you've got there. He's a real Summers.

He's got horses in his blood.'

Mr Summers's face relaxed. 'I'm beginning to see that,' he said.

'This must take you back,' Ernie Bell said to Mr Summers.

Mr Summers looked at Dot and Dash. 'It certainly does,' he said, walking over to the foals. 'I haven't been back here since the fire. I'd almost forgotten what it was like.'

Mandy watched as Mr Summers laid a hand on Dash's neck. 'I had a foal just like this one,' he said. Then he frowned at Dot. 'That little one looks a bit thin, Nick.'

'She's had a hard time,' Nick said. 'But she's getting better. Mandy has been a great help to me these last few weeks. Dot needed a lot of tender loving care after her birth.'

Mr Summers looked at Mandy. 'Hmmph!' he said. 'I think I'll want a word with that young lady.'

Mandy took a step back and bumped into Mr Marr.

'What's all this about?' the man said. 'We came here to finalise our offer for the farm.'

Nick's smile disappeared as he looked anxiously at his father. Mandy knew exactly what was going through his mind. Had he done enough?

'Well now,' began Mr Summers, walking across to Mr Marr. 'I think I told you I had made a bargain with Nick.'

Mr Marr nodded. 'You did,' he said. 'But as far as I can see the conditions haven't been met. Look at the place. It doesn't look like a working stables to me. Look at all that rubble over there in that field. Look at that ruin in the corner. And the creosote on that roof isn't even dry! There are ladders propped up against the walls – and paint pots – and the hasp on that stable door isn't even properly fixed. Look at it!'

With that, Mr Marr strode over to the loose box where Dot and Dash were and pulled on the door. The catch gave way and he swung the door open. 'You may call that good workmanship,' he shouted at Mr Summers. 'But I certainly don't.'

'Be careful!' Fiona called.

Mr Marr looked at her. 'What?' he bellowed.

Behind Mr Marr, Dot lifted her head and whinnied, alarmed at the sound of his voice.

Mandy watched in horror as the little foal pawed the ground and shot out of the stable.

She cantered across the farmyard, head up, eyes rolling. Nick lunged forward but Dash was out of the stable now, galloping after Dot.

Dot made straight for the open field gate and galloped through. Dash followed close behind.

'You stupid man,' Fiona shouted at Mr Marr as she raced after Nick.

'It's all right. They've gone into the field,' Mandy shouted.

Nick turned as he ran. 'No, it isn't,' he cried, racing on.

Mandy looked where Dot was headed – straight for the pile of debris in the middle of the field! Her head was up. She was in a blind panic. Dash had almost caught up with her. Now the stronger foal passed his weaker sister and raced on, trying to turn her back.

'Careful, Dash!' Mandy yelled, running towards the field gate.

Dash turned, and checked slightly, then he rose into a graceful leap and cleared the debris. For a moment Dot checked in her stride and Mandy thought she was going to stop. Then she stumbled, took fright and galloped on.

Nick was running across the field, waving his arms. Dash had turned and was coming back towards Dot. But it was too late.

Dot's head twisted, her eyes rolled as she saw the pile of rubbish in front of her. She couldn't stop in time. The breath stopped in Mandy's throat as she saw the weak little foal rise into a leap to try to clear the debris. She seemed to hang in the air for ever.

Oh, Dot, Mandy prayed silently, her eyes fixed on the little foal, *please make it. Please clear it.*

There was a grinding sound as Dot crashed down into the pile of debris.

Mandy gasped and held her breath, willing the little animal to get up, to trot on. But nothing happened. For a moment Mandy stood perfectly still. Her throat was tight. 'Get up, Dot. Please, get up,' she implored.

Nick raced towards the little foal. Dash had stopped. He came trotting towards Dot. She lay sprawled across the debris. She wasn't moving.

Mandy found herself racing towards Nick and Dot, the breath rasping in her throat. She felt as if an iron band had wrapped itself round her chest. *She isn't really hurt,* she told herself. *She'll get up in a moment.*

Nick turned briefly, his face pale. 'Get Dash!' he shouted and Mandy swerved, changing direction. She caught Dash by the bridle and pulled his head down. He strained at the bridle, trying to move forward, trying to get to his sister.

Gently Mandy led the foal towards Nick and Dot. Nick was kneeling beside the little foal. He looked up as they approached, his face as white as chalk.

Mandy swallowed. There seemed to be something in her throat, choking her. She could hardly get the words out. 'Is she badly hurt?' she asked, not daring to look. Behind her she could hear people coming towards them but they seemed to be a long way away.

Nick nodded. 'Very badly,' he said.

This time Mandy looked. Dot lay where she had fallen. Her eyes were closed and her forelegs were twisted under her. As Mandy stared blankly, the little foal opened her eyes and tried to lift her head. Dash whinnied and lowered his head to nuzzle his sister.

'She'll be all right, won't she, Nick?' Mandy said, biting back tears. 'Please say she'll be all right.'

Nick shook his head. 'I'm afraid not, Mandy,' he said. 'Not this time.'

Then Mandy felt the tears, hot and stinging,

sliding down her cheeks. The world swam before her and she dashed the tears away but they kept on coming, filling her eyes, choking her.

'But she's *got* to be all right,' she pleaded. 'She's fought so hard just to be alive.'

She felt a hand on her shoulder and looked up. It was her father. The others were gathered behind him.

'Can you take Dash back to the stables, Mandy?' he said gently. 'Grandad has gone for my bag. I'll do what has to be done here.'

Mandy look a long, shuddering breath. 'You mean put her to sleep?' she said through her tears.

Mr Hope nodded. 'It's the only thing to do,' he said. 'Her forelegs are broken.'

Mandy looked up at her father, tears streaming down her cheeks. 'Can't you save her?' she begged.

Adam Hope shook his head. 'Be brave. The sooner she's out of her misery, the better for her. She must be in terrible pain.'

Mandy swallowed, her throat raw. 'Can I – say goodbye?' she asked brokenly.

Mr Hope nodded and turned away as Mandy knelt and bent over the little foal. She laid her hand on Dot's neck. Tears splashed down and lay on Dot's shiny black coat. Mandy reached a hand down and gently wiped them away, feeling Dot's warmth under her fingers. Then she buried her head in the little foal's neck and sobbed as if her heart would break. She didn't know how long it was before her father touched her gently on the shoulder.

'Mandy . . .' he said softly.

Mandy lifted her head and nodded blindly. She didn't think she would ever be able to stop crying. She drew her hand across her eyes and laid it once more on Dot's neck. This was the foal they had looked after. They had fed her, encouraged her, nursed her – and all for nothing.

'What was the point of it all?' she said softly.

'There *was* a point,' Mr Hope said gently. 'Think how brave Dot was. Think of her running free in the field. She had great courage. You have to have courage too.'

Mandy bit back a fresh flow of tears, trying to be brave like Dot. She knew her father was right but it was so hard to accept. She looked once again at the little foal lying broken and in pain amongst the debris.

'I'll never forget you, Dot,' she said softly. 'Never.'

She felt a soft breath on the back of her neck and reached out a hand. Dash rubbed his nose along Mandy's arm.

'Come on, Dash,' Mandy said, stronger now. She laid her cheek against the foal's warm mane. 'Let's get you back to Bessie.'

Though her legs felt like lead she rose to her feet.

'You're a good girl, Mandy – and a brave one,' said a voice.

Mandy looked up. It was Mr Summers. He

was trying to smile at her but his face was pale like Nick's. Mandy couldn't speak. He looked down at his son, still kneeling beside Dot.

'It was an accident, Nick,' he said.

Nick looked up at him and shook his head wearily. His cheeks were streaked with tears too. 'No, Dad,' he said. 'You were right. I can't make a go of this. I was so anxious to get the stable block finished on time I forgot all about that loose hasp on the stable door. I meant to fix it before putting the horses in.'

'Anybody could have made that mistake,' Mr Summers said.

But Nick shook his head again. 'No,' he said. 'If I can't look after the horses I'm not fit to run the place. I'll stick to our bargain, Dad. You can sell Drysdale to the Marrs. I'll come into the building business. You were right all along.'

Eleven

'Sell Drysdale?' said Mr Summers. 'We'll see about that. Meantime, you've got a job to do, Nick. Here comes Tom Hope.'

Mandy turned to see Grandad hurrying across the field with her father's bag.

'You hold Dot's head while I give her the injection, Nick,' Mr Hope said.

Nick looked horrified. 'I can't,' he said. 'Not after what I've done to her.'

'Yes, you can,' said Mr Summers firmly. 'You owe it to her. This is part of rearing horses too, Nick. I'll help you.'

'Take Dash back to the stables, Mandy,' Mr

Hope said. 'And everybody else too.'

Mandy turned, leading the foal across the field. Grandad put an arm round her shoulder as they went. He didn't say anything. His arm was comfort enough.

Back at the stables Mandy spent a long time with Dash and Bessie. Dash was trembling so Mandy put a blanket over him and slid an arm round his neck.

'There,' she said. 'Bessie has only one foal now but she can be proud of you, Dash. You tried to save your little sister.'

'Mandy,' said a voice from the door.

Mandy turned. It was Fiona.

'Aunt Amelia has just made some tea,' Fiona said. 'Most of the others have gone but James is still here, and your dad. Come and have a cup of tea with us.'

Mandy nodded. 'I'll just tie up the stable door,' she said.

Fiona's voice was unsteady. 'You don't have to,' she said. 'Ernie Bell fixed the latch straight away – while you were over in the field. It's a bit late now, I know, but it made Ernie feel better.'

Mandy latched the door and followed Fiona into the farmhouse. Mrs Ponsonby was bustling around putting plates of sandwiches and cups of tea in front of everyone. Mr Summers, Nick, Mr Hope and James were seated round the table. James made room for her next to him and shoved his glasses up his nose.

'How is Dash?' he asked.

'Upset,' said Mandy. 'He looks so lonely without his twin.'

'What did you think of those Marrs?' said Mrs Ponsonby, sitting down at the table. 'Dreadful people. I had a terrible time getting rid of them.'

'You'll have to get used to them,' Nick said. 'They're going to be living here once they get their holiday home project set up.'

'Holiday homes!' said Mrs Ponsonby. 'Over my dead body!'

'It isn't up to you, Aunt Amelia,' Fiona said gently. 'Mr Summers has decided to sell to them. Nick knows we've failed.'

'Who says I've decided to sell to them?' Mr Summers said. 'And who says you've failed? You two have done a wonderful job getting this place fixed up.'

'But it was my fault Dot had to be put down,' Nick said.

'Rubbish,' his father said. 'It was that idiot

Marr. Opening the stable door like that and yelling his head off. If you think I'm going to sell Drysdale to a fool like that you've got another think coming.'

'You mean you aren't going to sell?' said Fiona. 'You're going to give Nick another chance?'

'If he wants it,' said Mr Summers, looking at his son. 'He's certainly earned it so I hope he *will* want it.'

Nick looked stunned. 'Of course I want it,' he said. 'But I feel so terrible about Dot.'

'Not half as terrible as I feel,' Mr Summers said.

Mandy looked at Nick's father. He was toying with a sandwich on his plate, not looking at anyone.

'What do you mean?' she asked.

Mr Summers coughed. 'I suppose you've heard about the fire at Drysdale years ago,' he said.

Mandy nodded. 'You tried to save the horses. Walter Pickard says you risked your life for them.'

'That was because it was my fault they were in danger in the first place,' Mr Summers said.

'What do you mean, Dad?' Nick asked.

'I had left a paraffin lamp burning,' Mr Summers said. 'That was what caused the fire. My own father was injured. He decided he was too old to start again so he moved to York.'

'You went with him, George,' Mrs Ponsonby said. 'I was really surprised by that.'

'I didn't want to,' said Mr Summers. 'I wanted to stay. I wanted to build up the farm again.'

Mandy leaned forward. Mr Summers was speaking softly, as if nobody else was there. It was almost as if he was talking to himself, reliving those events from forty years ago.

He cleared his throat and went on. 'When my father told me we had to leave I didn't feel I had the right to ask him to lend me the money to get the stables started again. The fire was my fault. I was to blame for those horses dying – and for my father being hurt. The memory of the flames, the screams of the horses haunted me for years. I didn't think I deserved a second chance. But I've regretted it since. I've often wondered what would have happened if I'd stayed – if I'd tried to save Drysdale.'

'But you didn't want me to do that,' said Nick. 'You were dead set against it.'

Mr Summers spread his hands wearily. 'I know

what a heartache it is, Nick. I didn't want you to have to go through the kind of thing you had to face today with Dot. It's the hardest job, you know.'

'I know,' Nick said gently. 'But it's what I want to do. I wish you'd told me all this before.'

Mr Summers ran a hand through his hair and Mandy noticed how like Nick he was.

'It must be in your blood,' he said. 'I didn't realise I was fighting that. The Summers always *were* mad about horses – and not easily put off.'

'Pig-headed is more like it,' said Mrs Ponsonby. 'I warned Fiona. But I've changed my mind about Nick.'

'Oh, Aunt Amelia, I'm so glad,' Fiona said. 'I promise I'll wear a proper dress for the wedding – and no gumboots!'

'I should hope not!' said Mrs Ponsonby.

'And *I* thought they were too young to get married,' Mr Summers said. 'I don't think that any longer – not after seeing how responsible they've both been – and how much work Nick and Fiona have put in here.'

'You called Fiona impractical,' said Mrs Ponsonby. 'As if a Ponsonby could ever be impractical!'

'How did you know I called her that?' said Mr Summers. Then he looked at Mandy and smiled. 'You know, Mandy, I think we've all got a lot to thank you for, after all,' he said.

Mandy blushed and her father laughed. 'I grounded her for a week for that trip to York,' he said. 'And I would do it again – but her heart's in the right place.'

'So you're going to give Nick a second chance?' James asked.

Mr Summers nodded. 'If he'll give me one,' he said.

Nick looked puzzled. 'What do you mean, Dad?' he asked.

Mr Summers drew a deep breath. 'Forty years ago I ran away from Drysdale,' he said. 'I want a chance to make up for that now.'

'How?' said Fiona.

'I'm going to take a couple of months off,' Mr Summers said. 'I'm going to come here to Drysdale and help you two get the stables going – if you'll let me.'

'Will we?' said Nick. 'Dad, that would be great!'

'Hmmph!' said Mrs Ponsonby. '*Two* of them. You'll have to stick up for yourself, Fiona!'

Fiona smiled, her eyes twinkling. 'Oh, I think

I can manage that, Aunt Amelia,' she said. 'You can give me lessons.'

Mrs Ponsonby's face broke into a wide grin. 'Come to think of it, so I can,' she said.

Mr Hope rose. 'I must get back to Animal Ark,' he said. 'Are you coming, Mandy?'

Mandy and James looked at each other. 'I think I'd like to stay for a little,' Mandy said. 'I want to spend some more time with Dash.'

'I'll bring Mandy and James back to Animal Ark,' Mr Summers said. 'I'd like to have a talk to you about buying some bloodstock for Drysdale, Adam.'

'I'd be glad to help,' Mr Hope said. 'And I wish you all the luck in the world.'

'Luck?' said Mr Summers. 'Hard work is more like it.' He looked at Nick and Fiona. 'Now, when exactly is this wedding going to be? We want to get Drysdale up and running before that!'

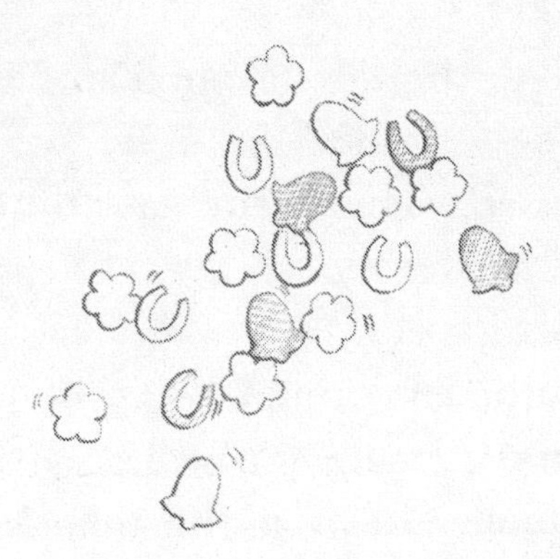

Twelve

The bells pealed out over Welford as Mandy walked out of the church behind Fiona and Nick. She lifted her head to look at the church tower. She almost expected to see it shaking, Grandad and Walter Pickard were ringing the bells so vigorously.

'Smile, Mandy!' James called.

Mandy turned just in time to see James snap a picture of her. Blackie was beside him. The Labrador had a big red bow tied on to his collar. *Everybody* had got dressed up for Fiona and Nick's wedding – even the animals. Pandora and Toby had bows in their collars too.

'You should be taking photos of Fiona,' she said. 'She's the bride.'

He grinned. 'This is the first time I've ever seen you wearing a posh dress,' he said. 'I had to get a picture of it.'

'But not the last time, I hope,' Mrs Ponsonby said. 'Amanda, you make a beautiful bridesmaid.'

Mandy looked down at the ankle-length pink dress she was wearing. James was right. It wasn't the sort of thing she usually wore – but once in a while she wouldn't mind it.

'It was really nice of Fiona to ask me to be her bridesmaid,' she said.

Fiona turned and came towards her with Nick. 'Who else would I ask?' she said. 'After all you did to help us.'

Mandy smiled at Fiona and Nick. Fiona looked wonderful in a full-skirted white wedding dress. She had flowers twined in her hair and a huge bouquet of pink roses. Nick looked extremely handsome in his morning suit – but a bit uncomfortable.

'I'll be glad to loosen this collar,' he said, tugging at his cravat.

Mandy smiled. Nick was much happier in old farm clothes.

'Don't you dare loosen that collar before the photographs have been taken!' Mrs Ponsonby warned.

Fiona made a face at Nick and he smiled.

'Anything you say, Aunt Amelia,' he said.

Mrs Ponsonby looked taken aback. ' "Aunt Amelia",' she repeated. 'Hmmph. Of course, now I've got a nephew!'

Mrs Ponsonby seemed quite happy about that. In fact, everybody looked happy. The whole village had turned out for the wedding. People were pouring out of the church door now, surrounding Nick and Fiona, congratulating them and throwing confetti.

'Well, Amelia,' Mr Summers said, coming to stand beside Mrs Ponsonby. 'They make a fine couple, don't they?'

Mr Summers seemed like a different person now. He was tanned and fit-looking from working at the stables with Nick and Fiona. The three of them had worked non-stop for the last two months. Mandy and James had helped out whenever they could.

Mrs Ponsonby looked at her niece and wiped a tear away. 'Just look at Fiona,' she said. 'She's so beautiful today – and tomorrow she'll be back in gumboots.' She shook her head and the flowers in her hat quivered.

'Mrs Ponsonby has more flowers in her hat than Fiona has in her bouquet,' James whispered to Mandy.

Mandy giggled. Mrs Ponsonby really had gone to town on her hat for the wedding. It had flowers, feathers *and* ribbons in it.

Fiona came over and tucked her arm through her aunt's. 'Come on, Aunt Amelia,' she said. 'Let's get these photos taken.' She turned to Mandy and James. 'Come on, you two. I want you in the photos as well.'

Blackie gave a short bark and Nick laughed. 'You too, Blackie,' he said.

Mandy and James piled into the back of the Land-rover with Blackie.

'Wow!' said James. 'Why did they have to take so many photos? I'm starving.'

Mrs Hope twisted round in the front seat. 'Hang on a little while more, James,' she said. 'There's food up at Drysdale. Gran and a few other ladies have already gone up there to get it organised.'

'Great!' said James.

'Isn't it a good idea to have the reception at Drysdale?' Mandy said as Mr Hope started the engine. 'Bessie and Dash will be guests of honour.'

'Maybe that will cheer Dash up,' James said. 'Nick says he's been pining for Dot.'

Mandy frowned. Poor little Dash had been much quieter since Dot died. He really missed his sister.

'Not just Bessie and Dash,' Mr Hope said.

'What do you mean?' said Mandy, leaning forward.

Mr Hope smiled. 'I think Fiona and Nick

might find a surprise waiting for them at Drysdale,' he said.

'What kind of surprise?' said James. 'Who from?'

'George Summers,' said Mr Hope. 'But I'm not telling you any more. Wait and see.'

'I hope it's a really *nice* surprise,' said Mandy. 'Nick and Fiona deserve something extra special.'

When they reached the farm Mr Hope drew the Land-rover to a halt and Mandy and James got out. Mandy looked around, her mouth open.

'When did this happen?' she asked.

The stableyard was swept so clean it looked polished. Fairy lights were strung across the yard, criss-crossing with streamers and balloons. They would look wonderful later on when it started to get dark. There were tables dotted around under the lights, covered in white cloths. Gran and some other ladies were just finishing setting out little bowls of flowers on every table.

'Look at that!' James said.

Mandy looked. There was a long trestle table along one side of the yard and it was heaped with food. Salads and pastries and all sorts of things.

'Who did this?' said Mandy.

'Mr Hardy provided the tables and the lights,' said Gran. 'Here he comes now. You can tell him how much you like it.'

Julian Hardy grinned as he strode across the stableyard with a loudspeaker. 'Music, for the dancing later,' he said.

'Mr Hardy, this is great,' said Mandy.

Mr Hardy positioned the speaker and stood up. 'This is my wedding present to Nick and Fiona,' he said. 'Do you think they'll like it?'

'They'll love it,' said Mandy. She turned as she heard a car horn tooting. 'That's them now.'

Fiona came running into the stableyard, looking around her.

'I didn't expect this,' she said. 'It's just like an open-air restaurant. What a lovely surprise.'

Mandy tugged at her dad's sleeve. 'That wasn't the surprise, was it?' she said.

Mr Hope shook his head. 'Wait,' he said. 'Here comes George Summers.'

Mr Summers cleared his throat. 'I haven't given you your wedding present yet, Nick,' he said.

Nick smiled. 'Yes you have, Dad,' he replied. 'You gave us a second chance with Drysdale –

and you've spent the last two months helping us get it into tiptop shape.'

Mandy looked around the stables. It was true. Everything was perfect now. The new stable block was all fitted out and there was no sign of the ruin that had been the old one. In its place Nick and his dad had built a covered exercise ring for schooling young horses.

Mr Summers cleared his throat again and looked at Mr Hope. Adam Hope nodded and walked towards the exercise ring. Mandy held her breath as her dad disappeared inside.

'I asked Adam to look out for some company for Dash,' Mr Summers went on. 'This is what we came up with. I hope you like them.'

Adam Hope had appeared at the exercise ring entrance leading two foals.

'Oh, Dad,' said Nick. 'They're beautiful!'

Mandy sighed. So this was the surprise. Mr Hope led the two nut-brown foals across the stableyard towards Nick and Fiona. And they *were* beautiful.

'One each,' said Mr Summers.

Fiona reached up and gave Mr Summers a hug. 'You couldn't have chosen a better wedding present,' she said.

Mandy stretched out a hand and the foal nearest her nuzzled her fingers.

'Oh, Dash will love you,' she said.

'He certainly will,' said Nick. He looked at his watch. 'The other guests won't be here for a few minutes,' he said. 'I'd love to see these foals stretch their legs, Dad. Let's turn them loose in the field.'

'And Dash,' added Mandy.

'Of course,' Fiona said. 'You go and get him, Mandy.'

Mandy hurried towards the stable block. It was warm inside and Dash whickered as she approached him.

'Come on, boy,' she said. 'Come and get to know your new friends.'

Dash tossed his head and pawed the ground.

'He's ready for a run at any rate,' said James.

Mandy stroked the foal's neck. 'I think he is,' she said. 'He's been so lonely these past weeks. I do hope he gets on with the new foals.'

Mandy led Dash outside. The other two foals were already in the field, racing each other, kicking their heels, running free. James opened the field gate and Mandy led Dash through.

Dash stood there watching the other two foals, uncertain, unwilling to move.

'Go on, Dash,' Mandy encouraged.

Mr Summers put a hand on the foal's neck and leaned forward, whispering to it, urging it on. His voice was low and soft. Mandy saw Dash's ears prick up. The foal shook his head, then tossed his mane. Mr Summers gave him a final pat and then Dash was off, running across the field to meet his new friends. His tail streamed behind him as he went.

'He's been so lonely,' Mandy said.

'But he's been brave too,' said Mr Summers. 'I've watched Dash over these last few weeks and he's taught me a lesson.'

'What lesson?' Mandy asked.

'Not to give up,' Mr Summers said. 'I gave up Drysdale many years ago and I was wrong. It took Nick and Dash to show me how important it is to have courage.'

'I think you've got a lot of courage, Mr Summers,' Mandy said. 'A lot of people wouldn't admit they were wrong but you did.'

'Thanks, Mandy,' Mr Summers said. 'I learned a few things about not giving up from you too.' He turned as the sound of car engines floated towards them. 'Here come the other guests,' he said. 'Are you coming, Mandy?'

'In a minute,' Mandy said. 'I just want to watch Dash for a little while.'

Mr Summers moved away to greet the guests. Mandy could hear laughter and voices. But they seemed to come from very far away. She watched as Dash trotted towards the other two foals. The brown foals stopped and lowered their heads, whickering. Dash tossed his mane and whinnied. Then, as if they had come to an understanding, all three foals began to gallop across the field.

The brown foals drew ahead then Dash put on a burst of speed and overtook them. He moved so fast that, just for a moment, it seemed as if there were two little black foals racing across the field together. Just for a moment it seemed as if Dot had come back. But that was only because Mandy had tears in her eyes. She shook the tears away and stepped back. Dash would be all right now. She knew that. He would never forget Dot but he wouldn't pine any longer - not with these other foals for company.

Mandy smiled. She would never forget Dot

either. And somehow, she thought, Dot would always be here at Drysdale, never ever growing old.

The Animal Ark Newsletter

Would you like to receive The Animal Ark Newsletter? It has lots of news about Lucy Daniels and the Animal Ark series, plus quizzes, puzzles and competitions. It is published three times a year and is free for children who live in the United Kingdom and Ireland.

If you would like to receive it for a year,
please write to:
The Animal Ark Newsletter,
c/o Hodder Children's Books,
338 Euston Road, London NW1 3BH,
sending your name and address
(UK and Ireland only).

ANIMAL ARK

Lucy Daniels

1	KITTENS IN THE KITCHEN	£3.50	❒
2	PONY IN THE PORCH	£3.50	❒
3	PUPPIES IN THE PANTRY	£3.50	❒
4	GOAT IN THE GARDEN	£3.50	❒
5	HEDGEHOGS IN THE HALL	£3.50	❒
6	BADGER IN THE BASEMENT	£3.50	❒
7	CUB IN THE CUPBOARD	£3.50	❒
8	PIGLET IN A PLAYPEN	£3.50	❒
9	OWL IN THE OFFICE	£3.50	❒
10	LAMB IN THE LAUNDRY	£3.50	❒
11	BUNNIES IN THE BATHROOM	£3.50	❒
12	DONKEY ON THE DOORSTEP	£3.50	❒
13	HAMSTER IN A HAMPER	£3.50	❒
14	GOOSE ON THE LOOSE	£3.50	❒
15	CALF IN THE COTTAGE	£3.50	❒
16	KOALA IN A CRISIS	£3.50	❒
17	WOMBAT IN THE WILD	£3.50	❒
18	ROO ON THE ROCK	£3.50	❒
19	SQUIRRELS IN THE SCHOOL	£3.50	❒
20	GUINEA-PIG IN THE GARAGE	£3.50	❒
21	FAWN IN THE FOREST	£3.50	❒
22	SHETLAND IN THE SHED	£3.50	❒
23	SWAN IN THE SWIM	£3.50	❒
24	LION BY THE LAKE	£3.50	❒
25	ELEPHANTS IN THE EAST	£3.50	❒
26	MONKEYS ON THE MOUNTAIN	£3.50	❒
27	DOG AT THE DOOR	£3.50	❒
	SHEEPDOG IN THE SNOW	£3.50	❒
	KITTEN IN THE COLD	£3.50	❒
	FOX IN THE FROST	£3.50	❒
	SEAL ON THE SHORE	£3.50	❒